THE SPIDER:
WINGS OF THE BLACK DEATH

WINGS OF THE BLACK DEATH

By Grant Stockbridge

ALTUS PRESS • 2019

PUBLISHING HISTORY

"Wings of the Black Death" originally appeared in the December, 1933 (Vol. 1, No. 3) issue of *The Spider* magazine. Copyright 2019 by Argosy Communications, Inc. All rights reserved.

CHAPTER 1
THE SPIDER RETURNS

RICHARD WENTWORTH, immaculate in evening attire, wandered with swift, deceptive carelessness among the night blackened shrubs, stealing away from the Police Commissioner's stately mansion. Behind him rang the gay laughter of society at play, but in Wentworth's eyes was only grimness and an alert watchfulness.

If those revelers knew as he did the fearful skeleton that leered at their feast, their laughter would turn to screams of horror!

Suddenly Wentworth checked his advance, halted behind the spire of an arborvitae. He merged with its shadow, quick hands turning up satin lapels to hide the white glimmer of his shirt. Just beyond the tree loomed the pacing figure of a policeman swinging a nightstick. But without pause, or glance toward the arborvitae, the bluecoat plodded on with heavy, heedless feet.... He would never know the Spider had passed in the night.

A wry smile twisted Wentworth's mouth as he catfooted on. This man was a guardian of the law. Because justice must wait on such men, Wentworth tonight had turned his back upon gaiety; leaving the side of the woman he loved, to grope through the vicious underworld in hopes of grappling with that mocking skeleton at the feast; risking his life once more that the tenta-

cles of crime might be kept from the throat of the city. Because of this, Wentworth tonight again became the Spider!

Silently as his namesake, the Spider sped on. A four foot wall of stone blocked his path. He rested his hands lightly on it and vaulted clear. A moment later he appeared beside a Lancia limousine parked at the curb. The chauffeur turned a turbaned head, and white teeth flashed in a dark face.

"Sahib," he murmured.

"To the address that you know, Ram Singh," Wentworth ordered and sprang into the back.

The auto muttered smoothly away, and, drawing the curtain, Wentworth fingered a button under the left side of the seat.

People died in the streets. Thousands fled.

The entire section—cushioned back, seat and all—swung forward. The back revolved and a neatly hung rack of clothes was disclosed by a small shielded light.

Wentworth's movements were deft. Off came the tail coat, stiffly exact shirt, collar, tie. He quickly donned a dark tweed suit, set jauntily on his black hair a dark fedora whose brim shadowed his eyes. He strapped beneath his arm a compact kit of chrome steel tools. At another touch of the button, the seat swung back into place, and the Spider was ready.

Wentworth caught the speaking tube and spoke precisely in Hindustani to Ram Singh.

"It is now," said Wentworth, glancing at his watch, "half past ten. At exactly ten minutes of eleven, Ram Singh, phone the police and tell them that the jewels stolen in the Racine case are in the possession of John Harper, the pawnbroker. Tell them then that the back door will be unlocked when they get there and that without a search warrant they may invade his office and catch him with the stolen goods."

Jewels. They had led many to their doom. But Wentworth had scant concern with them tonight. His wide information had brought him this knowledge, that Harper had the stolen goods. That bit of knowledge would serve to bring to justice a smooth criminal—and to prevent pursuit when the Spider had paid his visit.

WENTWORTH DROPPED the tube, seeing through the bullet proof glass that separated him and the Hindu, the slow single nod of the turbaned head. That was sufficient. Wentworth knew that Ram Singh would perform his task with time-clock precision. He relaxed into the cushioned luxury of the Lancia, drew out a cigarette and snapped flame to a lighter. He smiled thinly at its gleaming platinum sides.

Who would suspect that in this expensive toy reposed the seals of the Spider? Yet in a secret chamber in its base were those vermilion calling cards that had given him his name, that made the underworld cringe, and the police rage in futile anger.

Well, tonight he would need them again, would need once more to set police and criminals on his trail, united in their hatred of this master of men who set at naught the underworld's shrewdest plots; who snatched the criminal where police dared not go and left behind, to tell them he had struck, his mocking challenge—the seal of the Spider.

Wentworth snuffed the lighter, dropped it into his vest pocket and sat staring ahead with narrowed, burning eyes. Tonight was typical. In a bizarre combination of events too trivial for police to notice, the Spider had sensed the first outcreeping tentacle of a crime he scarcely dared to name, a crime that would blight city and nation for years to come. And because of that he went out quietly, with a smile, to battle with death.

It was the harder since the city, after drab years of depression, was just beginning to shrug its powdered shoulders free of the dreary cloak of poverty, beginning to laugh again and to sing. That night the police Commissioner, Stanley Kirkpatrick, had given the first really big, joyous ball of many seasons, never guessing the loathsome black wings of death that the Spider alone detected on the horizon.

On the surface, the crime which the Spider went tonight to rectify was a minor one. Virginia Doeg had been arrested for substituting forged bonds for genuine in the office of MacDonald Pugh, a Wall Street broker. She had cried out that she was innocent, that she had been framed. The Spider's first casual investigation motivated by the fresh innocence of the girl's face, which showed even through the crude photographs of the newspapers, had convinced him this was so.

Ordinarily, as Richard Wentworth, an amateur in criminology, he would have gone to Stanley Kirkpatrick with his information, set in motion the girl's release; but—there on the horizon were those sinister black wings which none but he had seen.

Three days before the girl's arrest, he had noticed a small story on the front pages of the newspapers. It stated that a dog had died of the Black Death, the Bubonic Plague, which in years past had killed its hundreds of thousands—killed them horribly with screams of pain and awful strangling, and blood gushing from their throats.

And that dog had belonged to Virginia Doeg, the same girl who now was accused of forgery!

Individually the two items meant nothing; together they might mean—Wentworth's hand clutched into a cold fist upon his knee.

He flashed a look ahead, leaned forward and tapped sharply on the glass. The Lancia snubbed down its nose at the curb. Wentworth touched the automatic that weighted his pocket, unfolded his lean height to the sidewalk, and—the shadows swallowed the Spider.

CHAPTER 2
"SPIDER, YOU MUST DIE!"

FIVE MINUTES later a passerby might have seen a black shadow slip into the entrance of a shabby tenement. Within the building dim gas light scarcely dissipated the darkness through which the Spider slipped.

Wentworth went on soundless feet through the halls and out of a door that opened on a yard cluttered with cans and refuse. He crossed it at an angle, muscled himself to the top of a fence and vaulted over, then crouched, waiting.

From nearby tenements voices gabbled. A cheap radio dinned into the blackness, and a sick infant wailed. Wentworth glanced at the luminous dial of his watch. Five minutes had elapsed since he had left the limousine. In twelve more Ram Singh's voice would summon the police. He crept forward.

Never was there rest for the Spider. He had been back from Europe but one day, but already this injustice, this hint of impending horror called him forth.

Wentworth's smile was slightly mocking. Yes, injustice angered him. He flew to the protection of its victims with such anger as a man feels when he sees a dog kicked viciously, or a dray horse beaten senseless as it struggles against a heavy load.

His mind flicked back to the case in hand.

Forgery of bonds—well, the Spider knew where that pointed. John Harper prospered by that racket. And John Harper's pawnshop lay just ahead of him, its back windows barred and forbidding, its heavy iron door a veritable Gibraltar.

The thin smile that the Spider perpetually wore in battle twisted his lips and he slipped forward across the shadow-blackened yard, threading a soundless way among tin cans and crates.

Before the iron door he paused a second, drew from the kit of chrome steel tools against his side a long, slender blade and ran this rapidly around the edge of the door until his sensitive fingers felt it contact the plates of the burglar alarm. Holding the metal grounded against that plate and the brick side of the building, he rapidly picked the lock and opened the door.

The Spider knew the secret of burglar alarms, knew that it was the break in the circuit formed by the plate on the door and the plate on the door-jamb—their separation by the doors opening—that caused the alarm to ring. So long as the connection was completed, grounded by that metal tool against the brick, it would not ring.

Swiftly the Spider slid into the blackness within and shut the door silently behind him. The tools went back into the kit against his side, and he drew from it a black silk mask that, fitting tightly across his eyes, hung limply down from there and concealed all of his face.

His left hand now held a small but powerful flashlight; his right the automatic.

Like his namesake, silently, the Spider drifted up old stairs that would have creaked aloud in protest against less able feet. BENEATH A door at their top a thread of light gleamed, but the Spider did not go directly to that door. Instead he moved silently along the hall, exploring it and the rooms that opened off it, and not until he found that they were empty did he glide back to the door where the light showed.

The flashlight vanished in his pocket, and with the gun held in his hand, he twisted the knob and thrust in the door.

There was a small squeak from the man who crouched behind the velvet-topped table, a tiny gasp of alarm, then silence. And the Spider, with the door kicked shut behind him, stood silently, his lips bitterly thin beneath the mask, and looked at John Harper.

The only light in the room was a low-swung green-shaded globe that focused straight down on the black velvet top of the table behind which the pawnbroker sat, shone queerly upon the man's prematurely bald head. A double handful of jewels glittered upon the velvet, and John Harper's fat fingers clutched them. His smooth, pink-cheeked face showed a mingling of greed and fear.

One of his hands moved slowly, slid along the velvet to the right.

"Keep your hand away from that button, Harper," Wentworth bit out.

Once more the quavering cry issued from the man, and he jerked his hand away from the spot toward which it had been traveling.

Wentworth's lip lifted in contempt. This man was a fence and a forger, to the Spider the lowest forms of all criminal life. He stood and stared at the man through the slits of his black silk mask. The edge of the light fell squarely on his hand, glittered on the leveled gun, and the two men were frozen into hostile statues.

Wentworth let the silence go on until it rang in his ears. He had time—ten minutes, perhaps. His eyes flickered to the huge safe at Harper's elbow. It was closed, locked, but such a safe would take only a few minutes for the Spider's sensitive fingers to open.

He waited and finally Harper, gathering all his courage,

squeaked out, "What do you want? You know you can't do this to me. I am John Harper. When *they* find out about this they will make you pay!"

A short, sharp laugh came from the Spider's concealed lips. Pay! *They* had been trying to make him pay for years now, and the Spider still lived, still nullified their cleverest plots, snatched from them their richest loot.

Wentworth took three short steps so that he stood only a yard from the table's edge.

"Listen to me," he said. "The bonds that were stolen from MacDonald Pugh's office, the ones for which you made forged copies. I want them."

Bewildered, embattled fear filled the fat sly face above the table. The high bald head wrinkled as John Harper strove to solve the puzzle as to why a crook with a gun should ask for bonds, when jewels sparkled beneath the bright electric light. But he dissembled swiftly.

"I don't know what you mean," he quavered.

Wentworth's body crouched forward, the gun advanced an inch, and his masked face lowered slowly into the puddle of light.

"Don't lie to me, Harper," he said slowly.

"But I'm not lying," the man said rapidly. "Honest, I ain't got 'em."

"Don't lie, Harper," Wentworth repeated in the same voice. "Don't lie to the Spider."

At those two words, "The Spider," the pig-jowled pawnbroker's eyes widened until the white showed completely around their evasive blue irises. His mouth opened and he swallowed audibly. But no sound came from his dry lips. He touched his tongue furtively to them, swallowed again.

"My God!"

There was grim amusement in Wentworth's voice. "Let me have those bonds—at once."

"But I haven't got them, I haven't!" the man cried.

The Spider allowed his eyes to flick to the safe, and the pawnbroker sprang into action, with an agility surprising for one of his weight. His fist shot into view with the ugly snout of a bulldog revolver. But even as he squeezed the trigger, the Spider flung himself aside and his own gun spat spitefully.

THE CRASH of the pawnbroker's heavy revolver was deafening. Lead whined past Wentworth's ear and lodged futilely in the wall. But the Spider's bullet had sped true. A round blue hole gaped in the forehead of John Harper.

For an instant he sat straight up in his chair, a surprised look upon his face. Then he slumped forward, his head spilling blood on the stolen jewels over which he had gloated. His life of greedy crime was ended.

The Spider whirled swiftly to the door, jerked it open. Outside all was deep, dark silence. No police whistles skirted in the streets; no sirens smote his ears; no one shouted. The acrid odor of gun powder drifted past his nostrils, and the Spider glanced swiftly at his watch.

He still had four minutes before Ram Singh would call the police. Four minutes before a radio alarm flashed out and swift two-seated cars sped through the crooked east side to seize John Harper with his stolen jewels.

A swift smile crossed the Spider's lips. No one would ever arrest John Harper now.

He closed the door and went swiftly to the safe, drawing on a pair of thin gray silk gloves. Then, with ear close-pressed against the face of the safe, he began to twirl the dial.

It took the Spider one minute to open the antiquated safe. It took him three more to ransack the compartments.

Dozens of documents were there that the police would be eager to see, but to the Spider they were unimportant. He skimmed rapidly through them, swiftly restoring to its place each document as he scanned it. He found no trace of the stolen bonds, but far down in a compartment in the lower left-hand corner of the safe, he came upon that which made his blood like ice in his veins. It was a glass vial upon the tiny label of which were printed two words, "Hopkins' Solution."

With the vial in his fist, Wentworth stared at the corpse of John Harper with eyes that held both fury and horror. Hopkins solution was the only efficient antitoxin for the Black Death!

He had been right. This man was involved in the framing of Virginia Doeg. Her dog had died of the Black Death, and in this man's possession was the plague serum. In Heaven's name what diabolical crime was being hatched here?

Swiftly the Spider stooped again and reached more deeply into the compartment. Other tubes of the stuff were there, and also there was a card on which were two names—Virginia Doeg and that of another woman, Mrs. Henry Gainsborough, of Roslyn, Long Island.

Rapidly Wentworth slid the card into his pocket, glanced at his watch.

One minute left. Time for the Spider to go. Swiftly he drew out his cigarette lighter. Swiftly he detached its bottom and pressed the seal against the safe door, leaned over and pressed again on the arching dome of John Harper's head. And where he had pressed, the outline of an ugly Spider showed in rich vermilion!

The seal of the Spider, his calling card! For a moment the Spider stared with his thin smile at the seals, then swiftly replaced the cigarette lighter in his pocket.

A slight sound behind him whirled him swift as thought. A voice drawled into the tense silence of the room:

"Just keep your hands like that, Mr. Spider."

In the doorway stood a tall heavy man, whose face, too, was covered with a black mask. In his right hand was a heavy gun, and its muzzle was pointed straight at the Spider's heart!

CHAPTER 3
FLIGHT—AND CHALLENGE

FACING THE gun in the hands of the masked man, Wentworth straightened slowly. His voice was entirely calm.

"You have me at a disadvantage. I'm afraid I don't know you."

The man chuckled behind his mask.

"You never will," he said. "It is unfortunately necessary for me to leave you here—dead."

"Really?"

There was mild amusement in the Spider's tone, but there was none in his face beneath the shielding black silk. Death glared at him from the slits of the other man's mask, from the black muzzle of that leveled gun.

Somewhere not far away Ram Singh was even then entering a telephone booth. Police would come. But they would bring no help to Wentworth. To the Spider the police meant death just as sure as that unwavering muzzle into which he looked. For there behind him in a huddled heap across the table was another who had paid the penalty for his sins. And the brilliant, small seal of the Spider glowed like a drop of blood upon his forehead!

Yet there was nothing of all this apprehension in the Spider's voice. He must play for time and trust to his split second reflexes, his keen mind, to yank him from the closing jaws of death.

"Curiosity," he told the masked man, "is an unpleasant thing to carry to one's grave. I don't know you, and I know most of the crooks of this world. Why do you seek my death?"

Once more the man chuckled.

"Simply because you have learned too much—"

Wentworth's eyes became pinpoints as he read the meaning behind those words. Then this man knew the secret of those vials in the safe, knew the horror at which they hinted.

"I don't know what you mean," he said. "Learned what?"

The man's laughter hissed into the silent room again.

"Guess, Spider," he rasped. "But guess fast. You have but a few moments left."

Wentworth raised a hand before him as though inspecting his fingernails, but his eyes shot to the face of his watch. Two minutes had elapsed now since Ram Singh had called the police. Any second would see them ascending the stairs. They might seize this man from behind, might interrupt this execution. But what would follow for the Spider?

Wentworth dreaded to think what might happen to the city should he himself be arrested now and placed on trial for murder. He might tell his suspicions to the police. But after all they were nothing but suspicions. And who would believe the Spider? Who would take his vague, unfounded charges seriously?

Wentworth's eyes caught the glint of electric light on moving metal and glanced quickly at the man who was his captor. The gun was rising slowly; he could see the increasing tension of the man's knuckles. The trigger was moving slowly back! And at the same instant Wentworth's straining ears caught the cautious tread of feet upon the stair.

The police had arrived; it could be no one else. Wentworth's body tensed for the final desperate moment. Then in the blackness of the hall, a voice roared:

"Hands up there!"

The Spider himself could not have whirled more quickly than the tall man in the doorway. Whirl and shot were instantaneous, and in the hall a man cried out hoarsely.

With a single movement of his hand, the Spider extinguished

the light. In two strides he reached the window, yanked down the top casement.

NO FEAR now that the killer would get him. Guns roared and bellowed in the hallway; lead sang and whined. The Spider smiled thinly as he fled. The police would take care of his recent captor now.

With swift, lithe movements Wentworth climbed out through the upper casement, planted his foot upon it as upon a ladder, and sprang upward. His hands closed upon the edge of the roof and for a moment he dangled there, clinging with aching fingers.

There were hoarse shouts below him in the yard, guns blazed, and lead plunked into the wood beside him. Wentworth flexed his arms, levered himself upward. In an instant he got a foot over the gutter, rolled and was safe.

More lead whistled by as he dodged away from the edge of the roof. He ran crouchingly across its narrow width, hurdled

—RICHARD WENTWORTH

the barrier to the next house, and, ducking beneath radio wires, proceeded swiftly across four buildings. Atop the fifth dwelling, he jerked up a roof scuttle and dropped through on light feet into the black upper hallway of another, smelly tenement.

It was the work of moments then to run swiftly down the stairs, jerking off the telltale mask and slipping it into the toolkit beneath his arm. And once more the Spider became a shadow, merged with the blackness of the lower hall. Casually he drifted out into the street and mingled with the excited crowd that was being pushed back by policemen from the danger zone about John Harper's pawnshop, where guns still blazed.

Richard Wentworth remained with that crowd until the police drove them away. Then, as if reluctantly, he moved off down the street.

Five minutes later, in a dank by-way, he slid again into the Lancia with a brief nod to Ram Singh. Then, as the imperturbable Hindu slid the limousine into smooth purring speed, Wentworth's finger touched once more the button that revealed the wardrobe behind the seat and he quickly garbed himself again in evening dress.

As he alighted from the car at the Police Commissioner's house, he glanced again at his watch. Nearly an hour. Too long—he should have been back half an hour ago.

Swiftly he moved, dodging again the pacing policeman and entered the conservatory. Standing in the doorway, he drew out a cigarette and lighted it with a flick of the lighter that so recently had implanted the seal of the Spider upon a dead man's forehead.

A dangerous thing for any man to carry—the seal of the Spider. And so Wentworth had found it in the past; but now his old friend, Professor Brownlee, had made him a lighter which was practically proof against discovery. The seals were there in the base of the lighter, in a secret chamber, but even that secret chamber would be hard to find; for a thin coating of varnish which matched the lighter, and which Wentworth had reapplied on his trip back to Kirkpatrick's home, concealed the narrow crack that marked the opening of the secret chamber.

In addition to that, if anyone but Wentworth opened that compartment, the seals dissolved in thirty seconds, for it was necessary to press a small hidden button and to bring the seal swiftly in contact with a surface to which it would adhere to prevent its dissolution.

WENTWORTH'S HAND, as he held the flame, was rock steady; he smiled slightly to see it, and strolled out among the guests. Nita van Sloan, the one woman he trusted in all the world, was whirling in the stately measures of a waltz in the arms of Police Commissioner Stanley Kirkpatrick.

The men's eyes met, and a wintry smile lifted the small black pointed mustache of the Commissioner of Police. He turned slowly in the rhythm of the dance, and Nita's quick eyes flew to Wentworth's face. She smiled, but in the depths of her blue eyes was a haunting fear.

It was not that she did not rely on the keen mind of her sweetheart; it was only that she knew the desperate chances he took, and the knowledge that sooner or later every man must yield to the mathematics of chance.

Standing there in the doorway, carelessly smoking as if guns had never whined bullets past his head, as if his swift justice had never taken life, Wentworth showed no evidence of his minutes-old tussle with death. What first impressed you about him was the remarkable physical alertness of the man. Five feet eleven, with the tapered body and light stride of an athlete, he had a keen, tanned face and the friendly interested eyes of a man who has long since learned the secret of enjoying life.

He smiled slowly, and even half across the room the magnetism of the man became apparent. He was so completely vital and alive. The music halted and he crossed swiftly, took Nita's hand and bowed over it, his gray-blue eyes smiling up beneath black brows that held always a hint of raillery.

"I have missed you," Kirkpatrick said.

Wentworth smiled lightly. "I have been communing with the stars. Libra, you know, is in the ascendant. That always brings luck—Libra, that is, in conjunction with Saturn—so I went out to watch my luck rise."

He turned smiling to the girl. His swift glance traveled over the bright turquoise of the simple dress that subtly emphasized the soft lines of her young body.

"Have I told you, my dear, how charming you are?" he asked. "A singularly trying color to wear, and you do it perfectly."

The girl blushed with pleasure, her face radiant beneath the clustering brown warmth of her curling hair.

"Really, Dick," she said, "and right out in public!" She turned to Kirkpatrick. "Isn't he simply impossible?" she asked lightly.

The commissioner's lips beneath the pointed black mustache were lifted by a slight smile.

"Dick Wentworth," he said, "is a man who does the impossible.

He took the cigarette Wentworth proffered in a platinum case.

"The stars have given me a message," Wentworth laughed,

"I have a feeling that the Spider," he waved his hand and a thread of blue smoke from his cigarette wavered slightly, "I have an idea that the Spider will be with us again. I heard stories in Europe that he was returning."

The Spider!

The words seemed to hover over the three standing there in the brilliant ballroom. It was like an Arctic blast in the midst of warm comfort; like a window banged suddenly open into a quiet drawing room, the storm and the rain beating in.

THE EYES of the two men met. Challenge was there, despite all the friendship between the two. Wentworth had once saved Kirkpatrick's life. There were bonds of admiration and respect between them, and yet in the police commissioner's mind was always a germ of suspicion. Many times now Wentworth and the Spider had been closely connected in circumstance and in simultaneous action. Always Wentworth had been able ultimately to turn aside that suspicion. But always it returned.

The girl's laughter at their side became strained and slightly uneasy, and the laughter was not in her blue eyes.

"Did the Spider, by any chance," asked Kirkpatrick softly, "come over on the boat with you?"

Wentworth threw back his head and laughed. "That man," he said, "he is so elusive. Who can say what boat he takes, what homes he will penetrate?" and he cast his gray-blue eyes over the rich assembly. "Why good Lord!" he exclaimed suddenly, "the man might even be here, in this room." He waved his hand again, and a tall man with forward-thrust bald head and eyes keen beneath heavy brows, walked over and grasped it.

"What man is this that might be here, Dick?" he asked and laughed—and added "Welcome home!

Nita seized on the diversion.

"Really, Mac, it's been ages since we've seen you."

"MacDonald Pugh," greeted Wentworth, "the great fisherman! Tuna will be running soon, Mac, and we'll have to go for some."

Kirkpatrick bowed to the newcomer, bowed again to Nita. For an instant a third smile flickered over his lips. "It was the Spider we were talking about, Mac," he said, looking at Wentworth. "I trust the Spider's presence, if he is here, will not cause you discomfort, Dick."

And Kirkpatrick, smiling suavely, moved away.

MacDonald Pugh looked after him with an amused smile.

"What's eating the old boy tonight?" he queried.

"Same old problem, Mac," Wentworth told him. "The Spider. I was teasing him about the fellow and, as usual, Stan rose to the bait. By the way, Mac, speaking of crime, you had a bit of an outbreak in your office recently."

Pugh's face lengthened so that creases diagonaled from his nose to mouth corners.

"A pity about Virginia Doeg," he said. "I'd have sworn she was honest. She was getting along nicely, too, engaged to marry a boy in the office, a James Handley. Intelligent lad, Handley, going places some day. And now—"

Pugh waved a hand.

"Good-bye to all that, eh?" Wentworth said musingly. "Usual thing, I know, that claim of frame-up. But I wonder if there isn't something to it in this case?"

MacDonald shook his bald head.

"Let's talk about something else," he growled. "Tuna fishing, for instance."

"I'll be by some week-end soon and make plans," Wentworth promised and Pugh nodded, smiled pleasantly and drifted off.

Nita's hand was quick on Wentworth's arm.

"Oh, Dick, Dick, why must you always stir up Kirkpatrick? He's convinced already that you're the Spider. Why make him sure?"

WENTWORTH TURNED his head, smiled down at her with his gray-blue eyes beneath his mocking brows.

"But my dear," he said, "there must be some zest to life."

"But to get it," cried the girl, "from hair-breadth danger, from laughing in the very face of death!"

Wentworth patted the small white hand upon his arm.

"Nita van Sloan," he said, "if I recall, has done a bit of laughing in the face of the gloomy old specter herself."

A pompous butler appeared in the doorway abruptly. Wentworth looked at him inquiringly.

"I was just looking, sir," he said, "For Mr. Kirkpatrick."

Wentworth glanced about. "There he is," he said, and at the butler's signal the police commissioner strode across.

"A phone call, sir, an important one, they say. Shall I attach the phone here?"

"Yes," said Kirkpatrick, and stood chatting carelessly with his two friends while the butler brought the instrument and plugged it into the wall.

The commissioner excused himself and spoke into the transmitter. Wentworth, watching him while apparently he listened to Nita's swift words, saw Kirkpatrick's tall body tighten, saw his hands clutch the telephone, heard his staccato words as he barked orders into the transmitter. Then he returned the phone to the butler and whirled. His striding across the room was like the charge of a lion. His eyes were hard as agates and his voice grated.

"The Spider," he said sharply, "has just killed two of my policemen!"

CHAPTER 4
"SHOOT TO KILL"

A THIN white scar on Wentworth's right temple, the relic of an old knife fight, turned red and began to throb. That was the only evidence of his excitement. His hands were steady; his eyes did not flinch from the stern regard of Kirkpatrick. Beside him he could feel the tightening of Nita's hand upon his arm, and knew that her blue eyes must be widened with horror.

Wentworth frowned slowly. "But that does not sound possible," he said. "I have never known the Spider to kill anyone except a crook."

"There is no mistake," said Kirkpatrick sternly. "That villainous red seal was printed on the foreheads of the dead men."

Wentworth's face stiffened with his effort at self-control. Truly this new enemy was proving a worthy antagonist. For Wentworth could not doubt that it was he who had placed the seal upon the murdered policemen. The threat of the terrible Black Death, and now this. Anger rose slowly within him like a white-hot tide. He felt his brow flush with it, and he clenched his fists. It was too powerful an emotion for him to conceal. He stared into Kirkpatrick's eyes, and his own pupils were pinpoints of rage.

"Now I swear to you, Kirkpatrick," he said slowly, "I will help you bring to justice the murderer of your men."

The Commissioner's face was set in harsh, commanding lines. "Remember what you say, Wentworth!"

"So help me God," Wentworth repeated, "I will bring to book the murderer of those policemen."

"Will you trap the Spider?"

Wentworth's mouth went into a thin straight line. "If the Spider is the man who placed the seal upon their foreheads, the Spider shall pay."

For long moments the men's gaze locked, and the slow languorous strains of another waltz came like music from another world, so foreign was it to the tension of the two.

Nita van Sloan laughed uncertainly beside them.

"For heaven's sake, Dick," she said, "Don't look so grim. One might fancy you and Stanley were enemies."

Neither man replied; nor did their eyes shift from their rigid regard of one another.

"I'll say this to you," Kirkpatrick said presently, and there was strain in his voice, "in spite of the fact that the Spider is a criminal, I have admired him previously. Admired him because he struck down the criminals that I could not touch within the law; admired him because he was fair and just. But I tell you now that this is different. That hereafter it is war to the death between the Spider and the police. I shall order my men to shoot him on sight—if ever his true identity is disclosed to us."

A slow smile spread over Wentworth's face. He had got a grip on himself now, and the slow red throb of the wound on his temple had subsided.

"I don't know why you tell me all of this, Stanley, but I think you are entirely right. I too shall shoot on sight when I spot the man who placed the seal upon the foreheads of those dead police."

For a moment longer the men stood face to face. Then Kirkpatrick bowed swiftly.

"I must ask you to excuse me now; there is work to be done." He bowed a second time to Nita van Sloan, spun on his heel and stalked off.

WENTWORTH LOOKED after him with a slight smile disturbing the equanimity of his lips, and mockery returning to his brow. He turned to Nita.

"Good old Stan seems to be a bit disturbed," he said. "Come, let's finish this dance; then we must go."

Nita van Sloan gave herself into his arms and they whirled slowly through the dancing throng. But her heart was not in it, and although Wentworth guided her skillfully and gracefully through the measures there was no pleasure in the waltz.

They took their leave then, and Wentworth, handing her into his car, said softly:

"Will you go home with me for a while, Nita? I must talk to you."

"Of course, Dick," the girl said from the depths of the car, and Wentworth, nodding briefly to Ram Singh, climbed in.

For a moment, while the car tooled through the traffic, he sat silently, the girl's white hand clinging to his arm. Finally the girl could stand the stillness no longer and broke out:

"Oh Dick—that awful seal. Your seal!"

"Yes," said Wentworth softly. "My seal. I think Nita, my dear, that I am entering the most deadly conflict of my life. This man is fiendish, utterly without heart. And he is clever." His fist struck suddenly on his knee. "Damnably clever."

In the darkness Wentworth's breath came short and fast, and anger rose in him again. The girl's soft voice at his elbow called him back.

"But what are you talking about, Dick? I don't understand."

Wentworth then told her briefly what had happened that night, and that his enemy must have placed his seal on the policemen's foreheads.

"Do you know what that means, my darling? If any criminal has the courage to imitate the Spider, to try to pin his crimes on him, then that man must have an amazing and fiendish plot before him, for the underworld dreads the Spider and fears him."

Nita laughed amusedly at his side.

"For heaven's sake, Dick, you talk as though the Spider were someone else."

Wentworth laughed with her.

"Someone else! Child, sometimes when I get behind that mask and go out with a gun in my pocket, I feel that no such person as Richard Wentworth ever lived." His fist clenched. "Nita, something so fearful that it will rock the world is in progress here. I know it!"

Mentally he was visioning the shadow of the Black Death just below the horizon glow of the city's lights. But why, he asked himself, would any criminal deal with such a fearful thing? What could he hope to accomplish with it?

THE CAR halted and a resplendent doorman opened the door of the limousine. Wentworth with a smile on his lips, descended and handed Nita to the curb. Together they walked across the sidewalk and through the elaborate, tasteful lobby, a man of the world and his friend.

Who would think that here walked the Spider, and the one woman in the world who knew his identity? Who could guess that this man was on the brink of battle with the most dangerous antagonist the world of crime had ever produced?

They entered the private elevator which lifted them silently to Wentworth's fifteen-room penthouse atop one of Fifth Avenue's most fashionable buildings. The ruddy-faced Jenkyns who opened the door bowed delightedly as he took his master's

NITA VAN SLOAN

cape, gloves and cane; for Jenkyns, his hair silvering with age, looked forward to the day when Nita van Sloan would be mistress over the household, when the dread pall of mystery would cease to dominate the young master he adored. His ruddy face was wrinkled with smiles as he hurried on to his pantry, to put together with his inimitable skill, supper for his master and the mistress-to-be.

Richard Wentworth did not pause in the drawing room, but led Nita directly to his thick-walled study. He seated her comfortably and gestured toward Ram Singh, who had followed them.

"A phone please," he said quietly.

Presently Ram Singh came back into the room with a portable phone and plugged it into the wall. Wentworth took it eagerly. "Have Jenkyns," he told Ram Singh, "get Mrs. Gainsborough on the phone. Mrs. Gainsborough in Roslyn, Long Island."

When the connection had gone through he asked quickly, "Mrs. Gainsborough? This is Richard Wentworth. Has anything unusual happened about your estate during the past week?"

As he listened to the woman's response, which grated so noisily that its rasping sound was audible to Nita van Sloan ten feet away, his hand tightened slowly about the phone, and his eyes took on an eager light.

"But Mrs. Gainsborough," he said swiftly, "you need not be afraid. I am not connected in any way with the police. I do a little criminal investigation work sometimes myself, and I ran across your name in that connection.... Yes, yes, perhaps you are right.... Certainly... I'll be out to see you tomorrow.... Yes, until then. Good-bye."

He handed the phone back to Ram Singh and whirled on light feet toward Nita. "Darling, the battle is about to begin. I want you to call with me tomorrow on Mrs. Gainsborough. I think she holds the key that will start the fireworks."

THE NEXT afternoon was sullen beneath lowering clouds, and the wind that stirred in their faces as Wentworth drove his swift Hispana Suiza roadster over the Long Island roads was hot and oppressive.

They swept from the climbing highway into a broad stone-gated drive and went on their way through trees up to the colossal columns that marked the home of Mrs. Gainsborough. The whole mass seemed to have been built with the idea of making a show-place, and the result was slightly ludicrous. Wentworth's upflung glance, taking in the whole facade, was mildly amused, but when he entered the house and bowed before the stout matron who received him, his manner was deferential.

The woman was absurdly overdressed, stuffed like a sausage into a too tight dress that showed too much of her pudgy arms for afternoon wear, and too much of her ample bosom. But there was no laughter in Wentworth's eyes as he looked into her pudgy face; for grief and fear were there, and Wentworth was no man to mock at human misery.

So Wentworth smiled sympathetically, and the woman smothered his strong hand in both of hers.

"Oh, thank you, thank you for coming," she said. "I have been so afraid." She managed a smile and sank heavily into a chair in the over-decorated and over-furnished room where she received the two.

She poured out the story in a swift gush of words, and Wentworth, standing silently before her, his eyes fixed in keen concentration on her face, listened with encouraging nods.

A letter had come, she said, demanding that she pay a million dollars to the writer lest her entire family be killed.

"A million dollars!" she exclaimed, and her hands flew in swift gestures. "A million dollars I have not got, or I would pay it willingly, to save my children."

She raised her voice and called out. "Marie! Marie! Bring Dave and Gertrude in!" She went on talking quickly. "This letter says if I don't pay they'll kill my children with—with the Black Death."

Wentworth started at the words. The Black Death. Then this was the answer to his fears, extortion under the threat of the Black Death! Good God! Who would not pay with that horror hanging over him? And this was only one case that had come to his attention. There must be hundreds of them. No man who could conceive using the terror of the Black Death would stop at one extortion. Wentworth felt the cold crawling touch of apprehension down his back.

Lord in heaven! If one of the victims refused and the Black Death were loosed, what would turn its fearful stride from the city? What would prevent the murder of thousands! Wentworth spoke swiftly to the woman.

"Have you the letter?" he asked.

MRS. GAINSBOROUGH lurched to her feet, moved awkwardly across the room on broken arches to a desk and returned with a crudely printed letter. It read:

> Unless you pay us a million dollars you and your children will be killed by the Black Death. If you agree, hang something red out of the upstairs window on the front. Remember, pay, or you all die by the Black Death.

Wentworth frowned at the thing. It was like any crank note, more than a little disappointing in its queer simplicity. But the Black Death—

A maid showed momentarily in the doorway, and two children came in. They were youngsters; the girl shy, with golden curly hair and eyes almost as blue as Nita's; the boy younger, with black hair and a chubby face that broke easily into smiles.

The woman's face softened as she turned and called them to her, and Wentworth felt a hand bite into his arm.

"Oh Dick, can't you do something for them?" Nita said softly.

Wentworth turned and smiled at her, and for a moment the alertness went from his eyes and they were very dark and tender. "I'll try, dear."

Somewhere in the house a bell pealed and the woman shuddered as she stood with an arm about each of her children. Fear came back into her face and her lips trembled.

"Oh," she said, "they called once before."

Wentworth's eyes were narrow and hard. "Let me talk to them!"

The maid entered with a phone, plugged it into the wall. Wentworth picked it up.

"Hello," he said, and as he listened his eyes sparkled with anger, and his fists clenched. "You keep well informed," he murmured. "Very well! But since you know I'm on the case, let me warn you. If you attempt to harm any member of this household, you'll pay with your life. Understand?" and abruptly he snapped the phone away from his ear, whirled to Nita.

"The same man," he said. "It's the same man. I heard his laugh, the same fiendish chuckling laugh as if he were gloating over something horrible to come!"

He turned swiftly toward the woman. "I'd get guards here immediately. He knows in some way that I'm here, so there's no longer any use of pretense."

He jerked up the phone again, spat a number into it, and began barking out commands to the police—commands which he knew would be instantly obeyed.

The woman sent her children from the room, and Wentworth heard her laboring feet ascend the stairs. He turned to Nita.

"I think it best," he said, "that Ram Singh drive you back to town at once. The man who just phoned declared that he was about to loose the Black Death upon all of us!"

CHAPTER 5
THE BLACK DEATH

WENTWORTH'S WORDS seemed to hang visibly in the air. The Black Death! It called to mind the drab, narrow streets of medieval London, visions of direful axle-creaking carts drawn by scarecrow horses; callous drivers who called mournfully, "Bring out your dead!" and carried loads of corpses like stacked firewood to pyres that burned like the campfires of a besieging enemy about the city; a stench of death and decay; smoke of the corpse fires that beclouded even the sun.

Wentworth stared unseeingly with horror-widened eyes. Surely no human being could conceive so fiendish a crime. Visions of that terrible plague sweeping through the congested millions of New York rose before Wentworth's eyes. Abruptly he jerked himself out of the preoccupation into which he had fallen.

Motors of automobiles roared outside the door and he crossed the room with swift, long strides. A dozen police rolled from the cars and, in charge of a gruff-voiced, waddling sergeant, straggled up to the porch.

Wentworth conferred swiftly with their chief and found him intelligent and competent. Twenty-four-hour patrols about the house were organized, and two policemen who would alternate were selected to stand perpetual guard over the children. A vermin exterminator was called in to destroy all rats and mice which might bring in the disease.

No food was to enter the house without rigid inspection, nor would any stranger pass the police cordon. Finally, satisfied with the arrangements, Wentworth went back into the mansion to give further warning to Mrs. Gainsborough against even a momentary carelessness.

HAD WENTWORTH'S thoughtfully intent eyes spotted a figure that crouched on a distant hillside and watched him through binoculars, as he entered the house, he might have felt some misgivings about the adequacy of the protection he had provided Mrs. Gainsborough.

But he did not see him. And on that distant hill a large-boned, skulking man with the brim of his black hat pulled far down over his eyes, chuckled to himself.

Twenty feet away from the man was a small black satchel with a screen for ventilation opening in one end; such a satchel as small dogs and cats are carried in.

For more than an hour the man sat waiting, propped up against a tall tree, while he watched the distant house.

Finally he saw something which made him chuckle with a gloating satisfaction that was horrible to hear. For from a side entrance of the home a small golden-haired girl and a chubby boy came out, gazing big-eyed at the blue-coated policeman who stalked beside them. They stood close-clustered for a while in animated prattle with their big guardian.

Wentworth came out, too, gave some final swift instruction to the guard, then strode off on an inspection of police.

The children began to romp and play upon the lawn.

It was then that that sinister figure on the hill put the glasses into their case and stood erect. From his pocket he drew an antiseptic mask, such as surgeons wear in operating, and fastened it carefully over nostrils and mouth.

Onto his hands he drew thin rubber gloves, which he wet thoroughly with an evil-smelling germicide. Then he cut a long switch and walked with wary eyes toward the black satchel. He picked it up and, holding it well away from him, made his cautious way down the hillside until he came near the boundary of the Gainsborough estate.

Swiftly then he unfastened the satchel, opened it, and sprang back; and from the interior leaped a small, bright-eyed terrier. It wagged its tail furiously and, bent almost double in an ecstasy of pleasure over its escape from the confinement of the bag, flung toward the white-masked man.

He slashed at it sharply with the switch he had cut upon the hill; two, three, four times he hit the dog savagely. It yipped, turned tail, and fled into the Gainsborough estate.

The man turned and hurried rapidly back the way he had come, leaving the satchel, and pouring strong germicide over his hands. He dropped the gloves and the antiseptic mask into a hollow tree stump, then continued his retreat up the hill. Once he had regained his vantage point he again used the glasses on the children romping upon the lawn.

He had not long to wait, for the dog, attracted by the happy cries of the children at play, penetrated to the lawn where they romped, and seeing them, ran eagerly forward.

It had been stolen from a home where there were children, and the monster on the hill, chuckling with sinister satisfaction, congratulated himself upon the thoroughness with which he had planned.

The policeman, he noticed, seemed completely unsuspicious. He patted the dog's head and allowed it to race and play with the children. And Wentworth was a mile away, checking on the guards on the opposite side of the estate.

The man on the hill saw this through his glasses and he laughed aloud with a rasping harshness, and, rising, vanished into the thickness of the woods.

WENTWORTH, STRIDING swiftly forward toward the Gainsborough mansion, stopped suddenly and listened. The breeze brought him the excited, happy cries of the two children. But it brought him also another sound that made the blood chill in his veins.

Not a sound to exercise an ordinary man, but to Wentworth, in that moment, it suggested death in a most horrible form. The sound was the sharp barking of a dog.

Wentworth broke into a pounding run, sprinting across the smooth green lawns with furious speed. Nearing the two children, who were playing with the dog and the heedless policeman, he sent his shout ahead of him:

"Kill that dog!"

The policeman whirled around, and stared at him with gaping mouth. Running, Wentworth had drawn his own gun. But there was no opportunity for him to fire. The children tumbled upon the ground with the dog, and only for fractions of a second was the animal's small furry body visible.

After seconds that seemed like hours, Wentworth darted finally across the last yards of space, pocketing his gun and pulling on rubber gloves that he had carried with him since first he had sensed the threat of the Black Death. With these he snatched the boy away from his laughing struggle with the puppy. He jerked out his automatic and fired two shots in the dog's head, then, without pause, caught up the boy and, holding him at arm's length, rushed back toward the mansion.

He called back to the girl to follow and the policeman trailed in bewilderment after them.

"In the name of all that's holy, Mr. Wentworth, why ever did you kill the puppy?" He panted, half trotting to keep pace with Wentworth. But he got no answer.

Wentworth increased his speed, dashed into the house and shouted for Mrs. Gainsborough. "Get the doctor here immediately. Tell him it's life and death! Tell him to bring Hopkins Solution with him, the antitoxin for the Bubonic plague!"

Wentworth forced Nita to leave immediately. He ordered the children put to bed, made them gargle with germicide and washed them and himself with medicated soap. And he ordered the policeman to take similar precautions. He did the same. But for the others, who had been exposed for some time to the dog, the precautions proved futile.

Never before had Wentworth seen the dread Black Death work with such fearful swiftness. Within half an hour of the time he had shot the dog, the children's faces had gone gaunt and yellow with the feverish touch of the plague.

The boy tossed and moaned upon his bed in a half stupor, whimpering with pain. Upon his upper arms blue splotches appeared, the centers showing the spidery tracing of blood-red veins, that dread marking which is called the Flower of the Black Death. Beneath his armpits and thighs purplish egg-shaped swellings grew. Wentworth touched one with the tip of a gloved finger and a scream of wild agony tore from the boy's throat.

"It's the Bubonic plague right enough," the doctor muttered. But the worry on his face was greater than even that dire announcement, with its threat to countless thousands, warranted. He shook his head, as he and Wentworth stared into each other's eyes with drawn countenances. "There is no record in history," the doctor said, "of the Black Death working this fast. The infection must have taken place four days ago."

Wentworth shook his head slowly. In the silence between them, broken only by the whimperings of the children, by the thudding of the mother's fists on the locked door, her broken pleadings that she be allowed to enter, horror raised its ugly head.

"I'm positive," he told the doctor, "that the dog brought the germ. This must be some new and as yet unknown form of the plague."

The little boy screamed out suddenly in anguish, straightened in the bed and doubled over its edge. Blood gushed from his mouth. The doctor went swiftly to work on him, and Wentworth made way for a trained nurse who had just arrived. Her skilled help would be of far greater assistance than his own. Somberly, he left the room, having almost to fight Mrs. Gainsborough to keep her out. He went directly to a bath where he stripped and literally bathed himself with germicide, syringing out mouth and nostrils. He burned the rubber gloves and giving what small comfort he could to Mrs. Gainsborough, entered his car and drove away. There was nothing further he could do.

He had failed, and the Black Death had struck its first, horrible blow. Wentworth's eyes were bleak at the thought of the menace to the millions of the city; the thought of a thousand throats echoing with those screams of agony that seemed even now to ring in his own ears; of a thousand bodies tossing in beds that were racks of pain; of a city demoralized by fear.

And over the entire city brooded that masked figure that was the Black Death—a masked figure whose hands would be red with the blood of the innocents....

CHAPTER 6
THE SPIDER UNMASKED

WITH THOSE deaths at the home of Mrs. Gainsborough began the most amazing reign of terror the modern world had ever known. Newspaper headlines flung the ghastly news at their readers in letters two inches high. Wherever people gathered in frightened groups on street corners and public squares, they repeated over and over those three grim words: "The Black Death." They were shouted above the clatter and roar of the subways, whispered in awed tones over the family supper table. Mothers glanced with worried faces at their children; and men went about their work with drawn lips and haggard eyes.

For the dread Black Death that had swept England, that had wiped out whole cities, had laid its horrid skeleton hand upon New York. It was fortunate the panic-stricken multitudes did not know, as Wentworth did, that the deaths were of human agency, perpetrated by a monster whose fiendishness was almost beyond belief.

The Bubonic plague had appeared in modern times before; it had killed its thousands in the East, but never had it been known in so virulent form as now. For the present disease was almost instantaneous, killing within twenty-four hours. And the form doctors had known and studied had an incubation period of four days. They had devised two serums for it; one which gave a partial immunity immediately and was effective for five days; another which acted more slowly but which was effective over a longer period.

Both of these had been used in the present outbreak and both had proved futile. Doctors spent long hours over their test tubes; laboratories worked frantically turning out the serums. But it was slow work and nearly hopeless.

Wentworth, lean-faced and burning-eyed, blaming himself for the death of those innocents, flaming with a white-hot rage against the man who called himself tauntingly "The Black Death," was summoned into conference by Stanley Kirkpatrick, the Commissioner of Police.

There was a never-fading scowl upon Kirkpatrick's saturnine face as the two men, sitting across the desk from each other, sought to lay plans for the capture of the criminal. But what information Wentworth had he could not reveal lest he also betray the fact that he was the Spider, a man now sought vengefully by the police for the murder of two of their comrades.

He could not tell him of the connection between that battle in the pawnshop, of John Harper and the gloating laugh of a man over a wire foredooming two children and an entire household to the Black Death, threatening the city's millions.

It was midnight when Wentworth left police headquarters and, entering his Lancia limousine, drove uptown with unseeing eyes fixed upon the turbaned head of Ram Singh. The car snaked through traffic, turned west to the poorly lighted streets along the waterfront, and Wentworth pressed the button that opened the secret wardrobe behind the cushions.

He rapidly extracted and strapped beneath his shirt his compact kit of chrome steel tools, dropped into his pocket a small but deadly automatic, and closed the compartment.

AT SEVENTY-FOURTH STREET the Lancia turned its nose east into a district of cheap lodging houses whose stingy light barely penetrated dust-filmed windows. Wentworth rapped sharply on the glass. Ram Singh glided smoothly to the curb, and, with a few parting instructions, Wentworth, the Spider now, strode rapidly up the street, eying the dimly revealed numbers of the houses.

He spotted the one he sought near the corner, went deliberately up the steps. The door resisted his skilled use of the lock-pick only a few seconds, and the Spider entered.

But this time the Spider was bent on no errand of justice; nor was he out to exact the penalty for some crime. The girl whose cry that she had been framed for forgery had won his sympathy lived here, and he hoped she might give him some clue to the master of the plague. But this was an errand that Richard Wentworth could not perform in his true identity. It must be the Spider who interviewed the girl, lest later inquiries by the police link the two personalities and identify them as the same man.

Up two flights of steps he crept, and in the darkness of the third floor his hand slipped beneath his coat and once more a black silk mask hid the face of Richard Wentworth.

At each door on the third floor he listened carefully, but found nothing suspicious. Finally he knocked lightly at the one which opened into the girl's room.

A pregnant silence followed his tap. But a moment later he heard a hesitant step and a feminine voice quaver through the thin board panel.

"Who—who is it?"

"Your friend," said Wentworth softly, "—the Spider."

There was a gasp and for a long moment more, silence. Then

a key grated in the lock, and the door swung open. The Spider slipped in.

He shut the door swiftly behind him. Before his masked face the girl retreated with slow and fearful steps. Her face was pale beneath the glowing red of hair that showered about her shoulders. Her hands clutched about her a cheap negligee of green silk, to which the fresh youth of her body lent dignity. Her mouth was open and a scream had caught in her throat.

"Don't be alarmed, Miss Doeg," the Spider said. "It is necessary that I wear a mask, lest my enemies in some way learn who I am."

His words reassured the girl somewhat and she dropped to a seat on the side of the shoddy white-iron bed which, with a second hand dresser and chair, completed the furnishings of her small room.

The Spider, with one swift glance, took in every detail, noting the drawn shade. He drew a cigarette case from his pocket and offered it to her, but the girl shook her head, with a small smile, and in turn offered him a box from the dresser beside her bed. A white box with gold letters and long gold-tipped Dimetrios cigarettes.

She laughed shyly. "My one luxury," she explained.

The Spider laughed, too. "Sorry I can't join you," he said. "But the mask—" He left the sentence in the air, and snapped a light for her.

When she had the cigarette going Wentworth began his questioning.

"Do you know of any reason," he asked, "why anyone should try to frame you?"

The half-smile which had hovered about the girl's lips faded entirely. She shook her red head.

"Do you have any idea why you were framed?"

"Not unless someone merely wanted to steal the bonds, and I was the most convenient person to hang it on."

The Spider took an impatient turn up and down the room.

"You work in the office of MacDonald Pugh," he said. "Who, beside yourself, would have an opportunity to substitute the forged bonds for the genuine?"

The girl's face clouded and her eyes dropped. But in the brief moment before her lids veiled them, Wentworth glimpsed something very much like fear.

"Come," he said sharply, "what is it? This is important. If you want to be freed of the crime, if you want—"

The door knob rasped slightly. Wentworth turned toward it. But the movement was amazingly slow for the Spider, almost as if he wished to be—too late. His hand did not even move toward his gun, and he stared calmly, a thin smile on his hidden lips, into the face of the man, masked like himself, who stood just inside the door with leveled gun.

A SMOTHERED scream burst out behind him. Wentworth, ignoring the girl, studied the slitted eyes that glittered at him through the slits of the mask.

The man advanced slowly, the gun in his right hand, his left hidden in his coat pocket.

"Over by the window, you," he ordered.

Wentworth said "Certainly," in a casual tone, as if he granted a minor favor to an acquaintance, and moved slowly backward.

The girl came again into the range of his vision and he studied her. Was she the innocent victim she pretended, or was she in league with the Black Death? The Spider had been certain after their clash in the pawnshop, that the criminal would seek to trap him. The only logical bait was the girl, and he had deliberately taken that bait, walked into the trap; for he knew of no other way to trace the man, and find him he must.

Otherwise the dread plague would stalk the streets; would lay its grisly hands upon man, woman and child—and the screams and meanings of the sufferers would rise to heaven like an unanswered prayer.

Wentworth felt the white thin scar upon his temple throbbing angrily. He knew sudden fury at the thought that this man, or his master, was responsible for the death of that curly haired boy he had snatched too late from his play with a plague-infested puppy. But the Spider forced himself to calmness, studied the girl narrowly.

She was standing tensely beside the bed, her hands clasped before her, shoulders hunched. Her red hair seemed to have drained all the color from her face. If she was actually in league with the Black Death and had deliberately betrayed Wentworth so that this man might trap him, she was as clever an actress as ever tricked a man.

Wentworth turned from her to the masked man again. The other's movements were wary, as he came forward toward the middle of the room now. The gun in his hand never wavered.

"Face the wall," he ordered Wentworth, "hoist your hands."

The Spider shrugged his shoulders slightly beneath the smooth fit of his dark tweeds, turned slowly and elevated his arms. A sharp cry from the girl, the sound of a blow whirled him about. But he was helpless. He only looked once more into the black muzzle of death.

The man bit out words, "I said 'Face the wall!'"

The girl was sprawled unconscious across the bed. From the man's left wrist dangled a blackjack.

"You filthy animal," the Spider rasped. "Why was that necessary?"

"Face the wall!" snarled the man, and the gun inched forward like the head of a poisonous viper.

The Spider hesitated. But once more he controlled himself, his muscles taut with anger. He longed to crush this beast, as he knew he could any moment he chose. But it was more important that he obtain a definite clue to the Black Death than that the injury to this girl be immediately avenged. He was convinced now that this man was not the arch criminal himself. Slowly he obeyed the order and faced the wall.

"Put your hands behind you," the man snapped and that, too, the Spider did. If he was to be bound, then at least his death was not intended now. He heard the man's heavy feet approach, and—lights blazed suddenly in his brain as a blow crashed against his skull. The Spider reeled against the wall, slid along it and slipped to the floor.

The man's knees gouged into his back. His wrists were jerked together and ropes bit into them. Wentworth felt the pain of the bonds. The blow had been no more than a tap behind the ear with the blackjack. He felt dizzy and sick, but rapidly recovered. Swiftly then he forced himself back to full control of his senses, for the man raised a slow hand and jerked the mask from the Spider's face!

Then jarring laughter rang in the room.

"So Richard Wentworth is the Spider!" his captor jeered.

CHAPTER 7
THROUGH THE FLAMES

WENTWORTH'S EYES held an ugly light. But he smiled coldly into the slitted eyes of his captor, and his voice was silky.

"It was unfortunate that you did that," he said gently. "Now I must kill you."

The man started to laugh, but his mirth choked and died. He cursed and struck the Spider heavily in the face. A stiff smile twisted Wentworth's lips. His eyes did not falter.

He knew now that his suspicions were correct, that this fellow was merely a muscle-man of the Black Death. He knew, too, that he had been ordered not to kill the Spider, but to bring him alive before the Master of the Plague himself. Wentworth veiled his eyes with his lids lest they show his satisfaction. He would permit his captor to take him to the criminal's lair, and then—Wentworth's eyes grew bleak....

Somewhere in the darkness of the halls Ram Singh lurked. He would follow as Wentworth had ordered, and together they would bring this Black Death to account. If only Ram Singh did not interfere too soon. Wentworth flicked a glance to the door.

The masked man took Wentworth's gun, crossed the room and crumpled some newspapers on the floor. He laid a chair across them, thrust the entire mass into a wooden, clothes-crowded closet and touched a match to the pile in a half dozen places.

Eager flames licked the paper, wrapped around the varnished wood of the chair; flimsy clothing in the closet caught up the sparks hungrily. Wentworth jerked to a sitting position, his head throbbing wildly. The man was calmly binding the girl's hands and feet with the obvious intention of leaving her to burn to death!

Wentworth's mouth closed in a tight, hard line. Even if it meant losing contact with the Black Death, he must save the girl. He got laboriously to his feet and inched forward.

The masked man spun with a curse, the blackjack ready. The Spider pretended to be dazed, wavering on his feet. The man struck—but the Spider was not there. Wentworth kicked out, caught the man in the abdomen and spilled him, writhing in pain, to the floor.

The Spider circled him, tugged open the door. "Ram Singh!" he called softly into the darkness.

No answer.

Once more Wentworth called his faithful servant, raising his voice. But his shout was absorbed into the blackness that gave forth no reply. The lurid glare of the flames tinted the shadows, revealed no sign of the Hindu. The masked man struggled to his knees, beginning to recover from the blow Wentworth had struck. The Spider could have run down the stairs and gained safety in flight. Instead, he stared past the man to the girl. The hungry flames ate nearer, towered until the electric light was dimmed, clawed at the ceiling.

Wentworth sprang toward it, launching a kick at the man's jaw. The muscle-man blocked it fumblingly, snatched at the Spider's foot. The grab missed. Wentworth skipped past him, turned his back to the fire and thrust his bound hands into a spire of flames!

His flesh scorched but he did not falter, did not flinch from the bite of the heat. Not until he felt the ropes give as they began to burn did he flinch away. His shoulders bulged as he strained against his bonds.

The masked man got laboriously to his feet, the black silk that covered his face gleaming redly from the flames. He reeled, recovered, roared an obscenity and charged. The Spider ducked under a slashing blow, and the man let out a shout of pain as he blundered too close to the fire and felt its singeing heat.

He whirled, checked a rush at its start and began to weave in more cautiously, wary on wide-placed feet. Outlined against the leaping, smoke-thick flame, his hunched shoulders were like a giant ape's. Wentworth retreated before his advance, fighting the ropes until they tore the flesh of his wrists.

Black smoke drifted like fog between them, blew its hot breath in Wentworth's face, stung his nostrils. He coughed rackingly, sprang backward as a blow glanced at his face. Still the ropes would not yield. Desperately, he fumbled in his hip

A corner of the coverlet already smouldered, as slow fire crept toward the helpless girl.

pocket, dragged out a cigarette case. He dropped it to the floor, set his heel upon it and crushed down heavily. The case shattered. Gray tear gas rose in a little cloud, scarcely visible amid the fire glare and smoke.

The other man's outstretched arms reached out to seize him, but the Spider ducked them, plunged across the room toward the cleared air near the window. An entire corner of the room was in flames now, and despite their leaping light the place was dark, blurred by smoke.

Behind him the muscle-man coughed and choked. Suddenly he tore off his mask and daubed at streaming eyes. But the tear gas Wentworth had released was not in sufficient quantity to put the man out of the fight entirely. The Spider had intended that cigarette case for use close to a man's face.

Shaking his head like a bedeviled dog, the other groped through the smoke toward where Wentworth crouched. His face was heavy, bestial, painted a lobster red by the flapping tongues of flame. Water streamed from his eyes. He blinked, gouging at them with his knuckles, finally spotted the Spider.

The man threw caution aside and charged, swinging the blackjack. Wentworth strained a final time at the ropes and a hand ripped loose with a tearing of flesh. He slashed out with his fist, burying it to the wrist in his adversary's stomach. It turned the blow of the bludgeon from his head, but the weapon crashed down upon his shoulder. Wentworth's lips tightened with pain, and his arm dropped limp and useless to his side!

WITH A lumbering charge, the man was upon Wentworth

again. The Spider smashed a fist into his face, leaped aside. With a bellow of rage the crook whirled and lunged again.

It was a one-sided battle, and only Wentworth's quick feet saved him from being instantly overpowered. The other was rapidly recovering from the small dose of tear gas, and all Wentworth's tricks could not overcome the handicap of that numbed left arm and shoulder. He could not block blows, could not fein. Instead he must retreat, duck and dodge, and get in a swift blow when he could.

Dense smoke and vagrant tear gas fumes smarted in his eyes, blurred his vision. The heat seemed to sear his lungs at every gasping breath. Good Lord! The girl! The Spider flung a quick glance toward the bed. A corner of the coverlet already smoldered, its slow fire creeping toward the helpless girl.

Abruptly, the muscle-man let out a shout of triumph. Wentworth's glance at the girl had cost him heavily. He was cornered! Fire licked out savage tongues to one side. Behind him, and to his right, walls hemmed him in.

Mouthing venomous curses, the man sprung forward and struck with the blackjack. No room to dodge. The Spider dropped to his knees. His right hand closed on something silken and hard in the corner. Gripping it, he lunged to his feet again, dived beneath another blow aimed at his head. He glanced down at the thing he had seized. Through smoke bleared eyes he caught the gleam of crimson silk. A woman's parasol! Despite the shallow gasping of his breath, the menace of the flames, and the crouching menace of the Black Death's hireling, Wentworth smiled—and it was a smile of triumph!

He now had a weapon. To any other man it would have been futile; to Wentworth it was perfect. He turned half to the left and faced his enemy along the line of his right shoulder. His feet were at right angles, the right pointed toward the crook, and his knees were flexed. He held the straight handle of the parasol across his palm like a sword, the ferrule raised slightly, pointed toward his enemy's eyes.

As the man charged in, the Spider thrust the parasol forward in a fencer's lunge, all his body thrown into the blow, his arm locked straight. The ferrule slid under the crook's chin, caught him squarely on the throat. The parasol doubled, snapped, but the charge was checked.

The weight of his own plunge hurled him backwards. He threw up his hands, staggered and thumped to the floor. The Spider sprang upon him, slammed home his fist. The head rolled limply over. Wentworth's hand went swiftly to the man's throat. The larynx had been crushed in, closing the windpipe and killing him instantly.

The flames' heat was fierce now. Long tongues of it crept across the floor. Smoke seeped up through the seams.

Wentworth sprang erect. Protecting his face with his arm, he plunged to the girl's side, slapped out the sparks that already had reached her negligee. He caught her up from the smoldering bed, put her by the window.

BACK ACROSS the room he reeled, caught the dead gangster by the collar and dragged him to the sill. He balanced the body, then allowed it to topple to the ground, a cushion for the girl. From the kit beneath his arm then, he drew a thin cord of silk. Padding this, he knotted it about the girl's body and, snubbing it around a bed post to ease the strain on his one good hand, lowered her slowly to the ground. He tossed the line after her.

Smoke streaked with flame billowed around him, but Wentworth, instead of climbing out, groped across the room and yanked open the door. In the street fire sirens wailed, men raised excited cries. Somewhere an axe thudded on metal. The Spider ran through the halls looking for Ram Singh, who, he felt sure had been overcome on his post of duty. Dark rooms and passageways yielded no trace of the Hindu.

Wentworth could wait no longer. At any instant now, police or firemen might crash into the building, find upon him the marks of battle and connect that with the man who lay dead in the yard. Kirkpatrick was sufficiently suspicious now. The Spider would do well not to direct the finger of guilt toward himself needlessly.

Wentworth darted to the back of the house, peered out. The girl was gone, but the crook's body still lay below. The Spider threw up the window, climbed out on the sill. Flame and smoke belched from the window directly overhead where he and the man had battled.

Feeling was slowly returning now to his left hand and arm. He still did not have full use of it, but he could steady himself as he reached out and caught hold with his right hand of a drain pipe. He stepped across the void and, taking a desperate chance, threw all his weight for an instant upon the grip of that one hand.

It was a terrific strain, but that hand had been strengthened by long hours with the foils. His hold slipped an inch but held until he could grip the pipe with his knees, then he let himself slide down, using his knees and his one good hand alternately.

When he reached the bottom, he leaned for an instant against the house, panting. But there was not time to rest. He crossed swiftly to the body on the ground and printed on its forehead the red seal of the Spider—a warning to the Black Death—and slipped away through the night.

He climbed a fence laboriously and, straddling it, suddenly was outlined in the bright beam of a flashlight. A gruff voice demanded, "Where the hell do you think you're going?"

Wentworth started to drop into the yard behind, but saw a second policeman bending over the corpse of the crook. The officer jerked erect, peered about. He spotted the Spider and a whistle shrilled between the man's lips. He grabbed for his gun.

Wentworth teetered to his feet atop the fence, crouched and sprang. Lead whistled through the air hungrily, but when it reached the spot, the Spider was gone. He had leaped high and wide and landed in the yard of the house next door. Another fence, running the length of the block, cut him off from the policeman whose light had found him.

Behind him a man's voice cried hoarsely into the night:

"It's the Spider! The Spider! Get him! Death to the Spider!"

HEAVY HANDS hit the fence, boots clawed at it. Wentworth ran at top speed. Necessity lent him new strength now. He swarmed over another fence, raced into a lodging house. In the street beyond more police whistles shrieked, and, "The Spider! The Spider! Death to the Spider!" men cried.

No escape that way; no escape the way he had come. The roofs? That was too obvious. Already blue-coated men undoubtedly were scaling upward to snare him there. He might battle his way clear, but the Spider would not fight the forces of the law.

He raced up the stairs, ripping off coat and vest. On the top floor he tore collar and tie from his throat and piled all on the floor against a brick wall. He opened his lighter, spiced its highly inflammable liquid over the pile, set fire to it in a half dozen places. Flames leaped up. Smoke and the stench of burning cloth filled the hall. Small danger of it spreading against that brick wall, but it seemed real enough.

Wentworth raced down the hall, pounded at a door. "Fire! Fire!"

He ran to the next door, beat with his fist.

"Fire!" he cried again. "Fire! Get out of here fast!"

Voices gabbled within. A door was opened a crack and a frightened, tousled head thrust out.

"Fire!" yelled Wentworth.

Other voices caught it up. Down the stairs he plunged and beat on more doors. The house was in a turmoil. People had been already awakened by the screaming sirens. The dread cry in their own building tumbled them out in panic.

Men with no coats, with trousers dragged on so hurriedly their suspender straps dangled; women in night clothes with kimonos caught across their breasts; young children laughing and shouting.

Wentworth tousled his own hair, let his suspender straps dangle, swiftly untied his shoes. He affected a limp in one leg. His smoke-swollen eyes seemed sleepy and his mouth drooped stupidly. In the midst of a jam of fleeing people, he ran to the street.

Police were clustered there, but the excited cry of "Fire!" broke their ranks and let the terrified mob through. Smoke was boiling out of the top floor window now. Police and firemen bounded into the building.

Wentworth stared stupidly up at the smoke, thumbed suspender straps over his shoulders. "Damnedest thing I ever saw," said the Spider with an atrocious accent to a man next to him. "Here I am sleeping sound and I hear the fire sirens making a fuss. 'Jeez!' I says to myself, 'Suppose that's this building.' Then they go on by and I goes back to sleep again. Then foist t'ing you knows here's this guy pounding on the door and yelling fire. Jeez! Was I scared!"

The other man shook his head glumly. "Me, too," he said, "And here I was having the first good sleep in a week."

Wentworth stared up at the building again, moved off grumbling. Nobody paid any attention to him and he eased into the darkened areaway of a building. The shadows absorbed him. He slipped a hand to the tool kit beneath his arm, and the iron grating yielded. It was the work of an instant then to penetrate the back yard, scale a fence and escape to the next street.

It was the heat of summer and a man without his coat was

not conspicuous. Wentworth shambled with slouched shoulders, but he moved swiftly. His car was parked where he had instructed Ram Singh to place it. Just beyond it was a Buick coupé, spotlessly new except for a rear fender that had been crumpled as if in a vise.

The Spider's eyes narrowed. He moved cautiously to the curb so that his own car interposed between himself and that other car. He stalked it cautiously. The Buick was empty.

But where was Ram Singh? A worried frown furrowed Wentworth's forehead. Never before had the faithful Hindu failed him in his need. Nothing short of injury or—Wentworth hesitated even at the thought—death could prevent him from coming to his master's aid.

With a dread that the prospect of death itself had not brought him, he went leaden-footed to the Lancia and tugged open its rear door. Two feet thrust out stiffly.

"Ram Singh!" Wentworth cried out.

No words answered him, but there was a muffled groan. The Spider's hand was swift to the light. It revealed the Hindu prostrate on the floor, bound and gagged, a gash across his forehead, but not—thank God—dead. An arm was twisted unnaturally and when Wentworth freed him, he found it was broken.

Wentworth sought no explanation, and Ram Singh volunteered none. Between them it was unnecessary.

"Did you see the man's face?" Wentworth asked.

Ram Singh shook his head slowly. Shame was on his face, but he met the Spider's eye directly, then began to climb slowly, with dangling arm, into the chauffeur's seat. Wentworth laughed softly, stopped the Hindu affectionately. He made him as comfortable as possible in the rear, mounted the chauffeur's seat himself and drove rapidly to a doctor, who was under obligations to him for a past and very secret service, and who did not mind winking at the requirement of reporting to the police every suspicious injury he treated—if the man he treated was a friend of Richard Wentworth.

CHAPTER 8
THE PLAGUE AGAIN

WITH GRIM amusement, the Spider read next day in the newspapers of the adventures of the policeman who had fired at him. First he had found a murdered man and an unconscious girl beneath a window from which smoke rolled.

He had carried the girl away from danger, and, returning, had found upon the brow of the murdered man the seal of the Spider! He had pursued the Spider and the man had vanished into thin air. Newspapers, putting the obvious inference on the rescue of the girl and the man's death, called the silken cord which had been found about the girl's waist a "piece of the Spider's Web." They marveled over its strength, for in tests it had resisted a strain up to five hundred pounds.

Wentworth grinned at Ram Singh, standing silently beside him with his arm in a sling, a little pale, but refusing to be treated as an invalid. A broken arm? *Wah!* It was as nothing.

"That's what comes, Ram Singh," said Wentworth, "of using

old silk. That bit of my 'web,' as they call it, should have tested up to seven hundred pounds."

But there was other news in the paper that brought not even grim amusement; that narrowed Wentworth's eyes with fury; that gripped his heart with cold fingers at the knowledge of his own failures to seize the Black Death.

For the Master of the Plague had not rested content with the toll at the Gainsborough estate. Once more the loathsome, strangling fingers of disease had clutched a family, and a millionaire's child had died with its nurse and mother. White-faced, Wentworth faced the conviction that daily, even hourly, the criminal was sending out his warnings, and where they failed, sending another message that carried with it death by diabolic torture.

And the Spider's sole clue to the Black Death was now in police hands—Virginia Doeg.

The girl had finally admitted to police that the Spider had assisted her and they believed she knew much more about that mysterious avenger's identity than she had revealed. They had her under triple guard at an unnamed place

Wentworth's gray-blue eyes glinted. That meant he would have to ask Commissioner Kirkpatrick to take him to her. He laughed shortly. Stanley would do it all right, hoping to trick the girl into some evidence of recognition. Once he had located her, Wentworth must in some way evade that triple guard, release her, and obtain the information he was sure she held which might point the way to the Black Death.

He first phoned Nita. "Darling," he said, "be very careful.

The Master of the Plague is out for me. Now his bait is in the hands of the police. He might try to abduct you for that purpose." His voice dropped softly. "He knows, dearest, as anyone must who knows me at all, that life itself is not so dear to me as you."

He smiled slowly as he heard the girl's eager rush of words, her fears for his safety. He warned her again, and left with a smile for the ruddy, anxious face of old Jenkyns, the butler.

THE DOOR of Kirkpatrick's office opened to him instantly. A new grimness marked the Commissioner's brown, saturnine face. The pointed black mustache, neat as always, seemed incongruous, like a butterfly on the face of a corpse.

He nodded without smiling, refusing to respond to this visitor's casual cheeriness as Wentworth offered one of his private brand of cigarettes and extended the lighter, which had always been a challenge between them since the day Kirkpatrick had searched the lighter in vain for the seal of the Spider.

"You have read the papers?" Kirkpatrick asked.

Wentworth nodded with a smile.

"The Spider, it seems," he said casually, "goes about his business as mysteriously as ever."

Kirkpatrick shook his head jerkily. "I mean the late editions of the afternoon papers," he explained.

"More of the Black Death?" Wentworth's mouth thinned.

"Yes," said Kirkpatrick slowly. "Old man Biltland himself has got it. Much good his millions will do him now. There are more of them every hour. Heaven only knows where this thing will end. Biltland came to me for protection after he got his letter, and now—"

"We must get this criminal, and get him quickly," Wentworth said savagely.

Kirkpatrick laid a clenched fist on the desk, his piercing eyes curiously steady on his friend's face.

"That seems to be the opinion of the papers, too," he said, "and they offer a clue."

Wentworth's quick question did not alter Kirkpatrick's curious stare. He spoke slowly:

"They say, and with strong logic, that there is a connection between the Spider and the Black Death. They point out that the two came to the city together."

Wentworth's small smile still lingered about his mouth. But he felt the slow beginning of a throb in that thin scar masked by the hair upon his temple.

"That sounds ridiculous," he said calmly, "as ridiculous as newspaper theories usually do. The Spider kills only crooks, and he has never been known to do anything for the money in it."

Kirkpatrick leaned forward and put his elbows on the desk, drumming with the fingers on one lean hand, his eyes still unwavering.

"Granted," he said. "I, too, find it hard to believe. Yet the Spider killed two of my men."

THE SMILE left Wentworth's face. He too, leaned forward tensely.

"For which I have sworn vengeance," he said sharply. "And that is why I am here. Take me to see this girl who last night saw the Spider. Perhaps I can get some useful information from her."

Kirkpatrick's fingers ceased to drum upon the desk. He stared fixedly into the lean, intent face of his friend.

"You ask me to let you talk to that girl?" His voice was muted.

"Precisely," said Wentworth.

For an instant the gaze of the two men continued locked. Then Kirkpatrick stood erect. A small smile twisted his mouth.

"Since you ask it," he said. "But in your place I would not have done so."

Wentworth's thin lips were mocking. "No, Stanley, I don't believe you would."

They went swiftly to the Commissioner's dark, powerful car, and behind a blue-coated chauffeur whizzed through traffic. Kirkpatrick turned his head and fixed his eyes upon the imperturbable profile of his friend. "We have her at a hotel, the Marlborough."

Wentworth raised his brows in amusement. "Rather expensive, isn't it?" he asked, "for a mere material witness."

Kirkpatrick did not answer, and the men were silent while the car sped on, The Marlborough on South Central Park, home of the wealthy and the celebrated! The Black Death would think long before he found her there, Wentworth told himself. Yet there was an uneasiness behind his eyes as they slipped on up Seventh Avenue past a blue-coated policeman at Fifty-Seventh Street, who stopped all traffic to let them pass and saluted smartly.

There was an unchanging frown on Kirkpatrick's forehead; and abruptly, as the car whirled into Central Park South, he slid forward to the edge of his seat, bolt upright, his hand a clenched fist upon his knee.

"Good God," he cried hoarsely, "What can be the matter?"

Parked at the curb were three radio patrol cars. Two policemen stood guard at the door and a crowd boiled about the entrance.

Wentworth jerked open the door, leaped out with Kirkpatrick at his heels and together they pounded across the pavement, ploughing through the crowd like a charge of cavalry.

"What is it?" Kirkpatrick snapped at one of the guardians of the door.

The man saluted, his face grimly concerned. "The Spider, sir!" he said. "Three of our men dead, and the girl is gone!"

FOR AN instant the news seemed to stun the two men, Kirkpatrick and Wentworth. They stared at each other, then ran into the lobby of the hotel, sprang into an elevator and were whisked to the tenth floor.

The hall swarmed with police, but a way was opened respectfully for the striding figures of the two men—opened to show them the bodies of two policemen on the floor, shot to death! And upon their foreheads glinted the blood-red seal of *the Spider.*

Wentworth stared fixedly at the seal. It was a clever imitation, faithful in almost every respect except that it was a little larger than the one he used. The two back legs of the Spider were curved a little too much also, but those trivial details would escape the attention of the police and indeed, if they were noticed, it would make no difference in their opinion of the guilt of the Spider.

A white-haired sergeant was in charge. His voice was bitter with anger.

"There's another of our boys in the room, sir," he reported. "And that makes five of them the Spider has killed. By God, sir, if ever I get my hands on him—"

Kirkpatrick nodded shortly, turned and stared for a moment fixedly into Wentworth's eyes.

He drew a hand wearily across his forehead, pushed on into the room where the girl had been held prisoner. The white-haired sergeant and Wentworth followed.

The Commissioner prowled about the room, flinching from the Spider-branded body on the floor.

"What happened?" he asked over his shoulder.

The sergeant's voice was still tight with hate. "No one seems to know exactly, sir. Nobody heard any shots. Nobody knew anything about the murders until someone rang for a bellboy and he came upstairs and found our men dead in the hall. They flashed an alarm to us and you got here almost as soon as we did."

"Then no one knows the time of the murders, exactly," said the Commissioner, meeting Wentworth's eyes again. "That will make an alibi rather difficult."

Kirkpatrick took a short stride across to the window and peered out. The building dropped away for ten stories straight down. He shook his head, turned, and looked about the room.

"What I can't understand," the Commissioner said, "is why the girl was taken away alive. Obviously this was done because, as I suspected all along, Virginia Doeg knew the identity of the Spider, and he was afraid she would betray him."

Wentworth slowly drew a cigarette and ignited it with a minute rasp of his lighter. He knew a different answer to this atrocity. He knew the Black Death had murdered the police and left the girl alive because Virginia Doeg was bait for the Spider, bait for a death trap into which he hoped to lure the one enemy he feared.

After hours of futile investigation Wentworth took his leave of Kirkpatrick and at once set about starting a new search for the girl. She remained his one clue, his one hope of lifting the dread terror of the plague that hung over the city.

Probably the Black Death would communicate with him in some way to reveal the whereabouts of the girl. Wentworth did not wait for that, for then the trap would be set. It was better to strike before his enemy was prepared. The Spider had a clue that the criminal would not suspect; a slender thread, it was true, but it might prove fruitful.

LEAVING KIRKPATRICK, he first went home and got the tool kit he carried only when, as the Spider, he went forth to battle the underworld. He changed also to special high-topped shoes, light as a fencer's except that they had thick, soft rubber soles.

There was worry in Ram Singh's eyes. Time and again the fingers of his good hand touched gently his broken arm in its sling as his devoted eyes followed every move of the master he had failed in his last grave encounter with the Black Death.

Wentworth straightened from lacing his shoes, clapped Ram Singh on his shoulder and went out into the night. He took a taxi directly to the local distributors of Dimetrios cigarettes, the kind which he had noticed Virginia Doeg had smoked.

It was a brand not widely sold, and its distribution would be confined to the wealthy, for it was expensive.

From the distributor he quickly got a list of the stores which retailed the cigarette, and went systematically about the task of visiting them all. There were fourteen in all, and he visited ten without results.

It was near the closing hour when finally he strolled into a small tobacconist's shop on upper Madison Avenue, purchased a pack of Dimetrios himself and fell into casual conversation with the clerk.

"Not many people buy these, I suppose," he said.

The young man behind the counter talked with a slight lisp. "Yeth," he said "that'th right. We keep them for a very thelect few. But you know, a little while ago, the motht unthpeakable ruffian came in and bought five packageth."

Excitement raced through Wentworth. Here, perhaps, was the clue he had been seeking. "Ever see the man before?" he asked.

"Never," shuddered the wavy-haired young clerk, "and I hope he never cometh back again."

Wentworth smiled slightly. "Tough guy, eh?"

"He wath," said the clerk. "He didn't even wear a collar, and had a mothst unthpeakable cap on his head and hith nothe—" He shuddered again, "Hith nothe had been mathed over on hith left cheek."

"Doubtless," said Wentworth, "a pugilist. And how long ago was this?"

"Jutht a few minuteth," the clerk said.

"You didn't happen to notice which way he went?"

The clerk stared at him. "Why?" he asked in a tense voice. "Ith he—are you—I mean—are you a politheman?"

Wentworth shook his head slowly. "No," he said. "I just don't want to go in the same direction the gentleman did. From your description I wouldn't want to meet him alone on a dark street this late in the evening."

"Oh!" cried the clerk. "Oh! Now I thall be afraid to leave at all." He moaned miserably, then he brightened. "Oh, but he wath in a car, that maketh it better."

"A car, eh? What kind?" Wentworth persisted.

The clerk frowned. "I'm quite thure it wath a Buick," he said. "But I didn't notithe the number."

Wentworth questioned him futilely a few minutes longer, then left, but with more confidence than when he had entered.

A ruffian who bought five packs of Dimetrios cigarettes. Wentworth felt a thrill of hope. He had not miscalculated then. The vanity of the Black Death would lead him to make just such a gesture toward his prisoner, to supply the particular brand of cigarettes the prisoner liked; or perhaps—Wentworth's eyes narrowed—perhaps this was the thread with which the Master of the Plague hoped to draw the Spider into his trap.

Wentworth shook his head sharply. No, it was too slender for that. Something more obvious, more certain of detection would have been employed.

But what to do now? He was in a fashionable neighborhood. Expensive and elaborate apartment houses raised their lofty crowns on every side. Where, in this habitat of the wealthy, would the Black Death hide a prisoner? In what sort of building could the ruffian he apparently employed find free and unchallenged entrance? How to trace any one Buick car among the city's thousands?

He strolled along inspecting the facades of luxurious buildings, many of their windows darkened now, showing untenanted apartments, since depression days had cut into the higher bracket income.

And abruptly the Spider smiled. Of course, that was the answer. Some of the buildings were closed entirely, purchased by big corporations for conversion into handsome apartments. They had been stillborn by hard times. Boarded up, they awaited prosperity and meantime stood vacant—perfect hideouts for criminals.

He crossed double-laned Park Avenue with its drone of taxis

and expensive motors, pushed on to Fifth Avenue, where apartments had been hardest hit.

Here in one block three such shuttered apartments stood. Wentworth had come directly from the tobacco shop to Fifth Avenue, probably the route a man searching for the cigarettes would have taken, and now, in the shadow of the wall that bounded Central Park, he stood and surveyed the looming buildings.

In front of a tenanted building next to a vacant one was parked a car that to Wentworth was vaguely familiar. He studied it and suddenly he remembered where he had seen it before. It was a Buick coupé, spotlessly new except for one rear fender that seemed to have been crumpled in a vise. That was the car that had been parked next to his Lancia the night he had killed one of the Black Death's men in the fire!

HOPE WARMED Wentworth. He started across the street, then caught a small gleam of light in the trade entrance of a building that was otherwise dark.

As he watched a man with a cap ducked out and, walking with the heavy rolling swagger of those who live by physical competence alone, strode toward the Buick.

Wentworth watched intently. He wanted to catch a glimpse of that man's face. If his nose was broken as the tobacco-clerk had described, if he was, in the language of that young gentleman, "a mostht unthpeakable ruffian"—a glimmer of a smile flickered across Wentworth's grim mouth—then the Spider would steal into that black-windowed building and deliberately enter the death trap the master criminal undoubtedly had baited for him.

Luck favored Wentworth. The man across the street entered the Buick with the crumpled fender and the dash lights showed the Spider the man's face. The nose was broken, mashed over on the left cheek!

Grimly Wentworth waited until the car had turned the corner, then strolled to the basement from which the man had come.

At a door he paused an instant, donned once more the black silk mask of the Spider and deftly picked the lock.

Quickly he entered and relocked the door. It made escape more difficult, but it prevented the alarm that an unlocked door might cause.

The Spider stole into the shadows, cat-footed to the stairs and mounted with the same sure competence. He went systematically about the tedious task of finding which of the many apartments concealed the Black Death and his prisoner, who, Wentworth was sure, must be hidden somewhere in this building.

He went from floor to floor, listening at doors, searching with minute gleams of his flashlight the dusty hallways for indications of recent passage.

Not until he reached the very top floor did he discover the trace he sought. There, mingling with the stuffy unventilated air, he caught the distinct odor of tobacco.

The Spider moved more tensely now, automatic in hand, every muscle, every sense, alert. The darkness was absolute. No vagrant gleam of street light could penetrate; no ray beneath a door betrayed the hiding place of the Black Death; no sound broke the tomblike silence.

Wentworth strained his ears, but there was no mutter of voices to guide him. The vast waiting stillness seemed to crowd close as if the very air were hostile.

Yet somewhere on this floor was human presence. Here, if anywhere in this building, the jaws of the Black Death's trap gaped open.

SOFTLY THE Spider went through the search that had become routine now, listening at each door. At last his ear caught the faint sound of movement within a room, and a thin smile twisted his lips beneath the mask.

The door to the trap was beneath his hand.

Wentworth turned from it and stole to stairs that led upward, unfastened a door to the roof, and searched swiftly for other ingress to the apartment below.

Once more fortune—this time a fire escape ladder—favored him. And because it did, he was suspicious. Things were too easy.

Yet there was a chance the Plague Master was not yet ready, that the hair-trigger spring of the trap did not yet await his cautious foot.

Once more a grim smile played across his mouth. Others had trapped the Spider, and found it a dangerous pastime. He descended the fire escape ladder that led down past the window of the apartment where lurked the Black Death.

Yet even in that he exercised care an ordinary man would not have thought of. He did not tread upon the rounds of the ladder but, taking his automatic between his teeth, gripped the sides of the iron stairway with knees and arms and glided down, lest an alarm had been connected with those rungs.

Wentworth's thick rubber soles made no sound on the iron grilling of the fire escape platform. He examined the windows. He could make out the shadow of heavy drapes, but no faint gleam of light escaped.

From the invaluable kit of tools beneath his arm he took out a small vial made of wax, and with a plunger attached to the stopper drew a semi-circle on the glass above the window's fastening. Hydrofluoric acid, such as etchers use. Soft wax was impervious to it, yet it ate like fire through hardened glass.

Wentworth replaced the wax bottle and took out a rubber suction cup which he fastened to the pane. When the acid had eaten through, he removed the piece of glass, soundlessly.

For long moments Wentworth listened at the opening, and presently his straining ears made out the slow deep breathing of one who slept.

Was it possible that he had taken unaware the Black Death? Blood throbbed slowly in his temples. He had moved swiftly. Within a few hours of the girl's disappearance he had tracked the man down. Probably no such swift action had been expected. It was possible that within this room the Black Death slept!

Without a sound the Spider eased open the fastening, inched up the sash until it was high enough to admit his body.

He drew his revolver, caught up the small flashlight in his left hand, and smothering the light in his palms, stared fixedly at it for a few seconds until the pupils of his eyes became accustomed to the glare, lest bursting into a lighted room would dazzle him.

Silently he eased himself through the opening, stood erect upon the inner sill within the black drapes that covered it. Then, tearing them apart, he sprang into the room.

His gun was ready, but firing, he found, would have been futile. Behind a metal closet door peering through a peephole of bullet proof glass, crouched a man, and the muzzle of his gun was trained on the Spider's breast.

Spring backward? No chance of that. The window was opened only narrowly; and before he could roll through, half a dozen steel-jacketed bullets could rip the life from his body.

Charge? The shield of the door completely protected the gunman. Swiftly the Spider's eyes flickered over the room. It was barely furnished. On a bed nearby, her clothing disheveled, lay Virginia Doeg, eyes closed, her red hair a veil over her pillow. It was her deep breathing that had deceived him.

And now the man behind the shield chuckled gloatingly. "Welcome, Spider!" he jeered, "Welcome to the death trap!"

Wentworth straightened out of his crouch, his eyes calm.

"Better drop the gun, Spider," the criminal said softly. "I do not think that I care to deal with you while you are armed. You should not have waited so long after you opened the window. Those drapes permit no light to escape, but they are light and the slightest breath of air makes them quiver."

Wentworth let his gun fall.

"Now back three paces," the man ordered.

And when the Spider had obeyed, the other came out from behind the metal door.

"It is not my intention," the man sneered, "to kill you at once. I would rather leave that to my amiable friends, the police. I think that even they will be able to capture the Spider if I put a bullet say, through his lung, and tell them where to find him.

"And you needn't fear that they will be unable to identify you as the Spider. I have a cigarette lighter myself, not half so clever as your own, which will readily yield up the secret of those little red seals to the police.

"If anything further is needed I shall murder the young lady who lies on the bed there—Unfortunate that she is drugged and cannot hear us, eh?—place that ugly little Spider upon her forehead and let them assume that it was she who wounded you, and that then the Spider, in the excess of his fury, managed to strangle the life from his so beautiful betrayer."

The man chuckled once more, gloatingly, behind his mask.

"But already we have delayed too long. The Black Death must be about his work. And you must be accounted for first."

He lifted the pistol, leveled it at Wentworth's chest and slowly began to press the trigger.

CHAPTER 9
THE VOICE ON THE WIRE

IN HER penthouse apartment, high up on Riverside Drive, overlooking the misty Hudson which she loved to paint,

Nita van Sloan sat upon a window seat and stared unseeingly out into the darkness of the night.

Far out on the bosom of the Hudson gleamed the pale yellow lights of passing boats. The black Jersey shore was shrouded in mist, a delicate problem for any artist's brush. But Nita van Sloan saw none of that. For all the deep cushioned comfort of the window seat, she sat tensely, chin resting on her palm. It was far past midnight, but sleep would not come to the troubled girl.

Lying beside her on the floor, the Great Dane dog that Dick Wentworth had given her as a puppy stared up at her with worshiping eyes, its nose outstretched upon its forepaws

Nita sighed deeply, and the dog rose with a low whine in its throat, and rested its head in the girl's lap.

The girl's blue eyes were tired as she turned them upon the dog. She smiled faintly.

"Are you worried, too, Apollo, about our Dick?" she asked.

The dog emitted a small coughing bark. It was his invariable response to the name of the master he loved.

The girl swung back her pajama-clad legs to the floor and strode nervously to a small table. She picked up a cigarette and ignited it. A moment later she tossed it away and moved restively about the room, changing the position of a picture, picking up a hair pin from the floor, doing a dozen things without thought.

For she knew that Richard Wentworth never before had crossed blades with so dangerous an antagonist as the Black Death. Swiftly Nita came to a decision. Phoning would be useless. He would only laugh at her fears, cajole her into remaining—and waiting—alone. And tonight she wanted warmer solace than that. She tore off the pajamas as if they strangled her, dressed with swift speed, and snapping a leash upon Apollo's collar, left the building.

In the pocket of her sport-suit she carried a small but deadly gun Dick had given her. She summoned a taxi, and entering it gave in a low voice the number of Wentworth's apartment house.

Her touch of the bell of his penthouse had hardly sounded the buzzer before the door swung open and the haggard face of gray-haired old Jenkyns stared out.

The smiles that usually wreathed his ruddy countenance were missing. Nita felt her heart contract.

"Then Dick—Dick isn't home?" she asked.

Jenkyns shook his old head slowly, stepped aside for her to enter. Apollo, released, bounded ahead through the apartment, snuffing excitedly. But presently he returned and crowded close against Nita as she stood in the luxuriously furnished drawing room, looking about with vacant eyes.

"Ram Singh?" she asked.

Once more Jenkyns shook his head, and Nita's hopes sank again. "They didn't leave together, Miss Nita. Ram Singh went out a little while after the master." Ram Singh had a broken arm, and a man couldn't fight with his arm in splints, Nita thought. Listlessly she tugged her brown hat from her gleaming, curly head and walked slowly toward a window.

Abruptly she was tense again, for from the hall sounded the

metallic buzz of the phone. She raced to it, snatched up the receiver.

"Richard Wentworth's apartment," she said, her words trembling with hope.

THE VOICE that came over the wire was not Dick's. It had a soft sibilance that made Nita's hand tighten about the receiver, that made a chill of dread race down her spine.

"Ah, Miss van Sloan," said the voice on the wire, "I thought I could find you there after I called your own apartment vainly. Richard Wentworth—the Spider—is my prisoner."

A gasp shuddered from the girl. Someone had penetrated the secret that no one save those who battled for him knew. Someone had discovered that Richard Wentworth was the Spider! And that someone—she was suddenly sure was the Black Death!

"What do you want?" she demanded, striving to drive the fear from her tone.

"Ah," said the voice, "I see that you are reasonable. That is fortunate. I was about to kill the Spider, but learning his identity I remembered that he was a wealthy man—and money is very dear to me. If you would care to ransom him—"

"Oh yes, yes!" Nita cried.

Evil laughter taunted her. "It will not be so simple as that. You cannot come with the police and liberate your—friend. For there is a little safety device which I have arranged to protect myself.

"In the Spider's pocket is a cigarette lighter that is a twin to his own in every respect save one. In this one the seal of the

Spider will not dissolve when it is opened, and the secret chamber is so clumsily hidden that even the dull-witted police can discover it."

Nita heard that news with sinking heart.

"You doubtless know," the Black Death went on, "where you can get hold of considerable money."

Yes, Nita did know. There was a safe in Dick's room where he always kept a large quantity of cash on hand against the possible necessity of flight that ever hung above his head.

"Get this money, then," the man ordered. "Come to the corner of Madison Avenue and Fifty-Seventh Street and walk uptown. Obey the man who meets you there."

Then reed-like over the phone Nita caught a faint voice as if someone shouted from a distance, and she thrilled as she recognized the voice of Dick Wentworth.

"No, Nita! No! It—means—death!"

A curse snarled from the man at the phone. She heard a jar, silence, then the dread voice purred once more in her ear.

"It was unfortunately necessary for me to silence your—friend. He is unduly suspicious, and a trifle troublesome. It may be that unless you hurry I shall be forced to deal firmly with him before you can get here. In fact I can allow you only twenty minutes. Remember—" the man's voice rose suddenly in sharp warning—"if you bring the police, they will learn that Richard Wentworth is the Spider. They will not forget that the seal of the Spider has been printed on the brow of five of their dead comrades."

"Oh tell, tell me," cried Nita, "that Dick is all right. You haven't hurt him—"

Over the wires came only a sinister laugh.

Nita put the telephone down with a listless hand. The anxious Jenkyns was at her elbow. "What is it, Miss Nita?"

She told him rapidly all that she knew, and the butler, too, begged her not to go.

"If Master Dick is captured," he reassured her, "you may be sure he wanted to be. And if he wanted to be, he has a way out. You'd only upset his plans."

The girl stared at Jenkyns. Dick Wentworth never went into danger unprepared, yet his cry over the wire: "It means death!"

She shook her head sharply. "Not this time, Jenkyns," she said. "You don't know what a terrible thing he is fighting, how clever the Black Death is!"

SHE TURNED swiftly to the task she had set for herself. The weight of the automatic in her pocket swayed against her side and lent a certain comfort. From the wall safe in Wentworth's room she took two hundred and fifty thousand dollars, made a bundle of it under her arm. Apollo followed her every footstep, claws patting on the floor.

She looked down at him. Apollo had helped her in many a tight scrape. But how could she use the Great Dane now? Dick had taught the dog many tricks, had trained him to pretend hostility toward herself if she made a certain signal. It was an old smuggler's trick. Frequently their jewel-smuggling pets were captured by officers who then sought to identify the master through the dog. And the man trained the animals so that they would snarl even at the hand they loved if they received a certain signal from their master.

Perhaps it might serve her in good stead now. She spun toward Jenkyns, smiled at him.

"Jenkyns," she said, "we are going to do what we can to save Dick. I want you to help me."

"Anything, *anything, Miss Nita!* But I'm afraid these old hands have long since passed the time...."

Nita shook her head sharply. "No, not that," she said. "What I want you to do is this. I'm going to drive Dick's roadster uptown to the spot where they want me to meet this man. I want you to get in a taxi with Apollo and follow me.

"When I meet someone, just let Apollo out. That is all. But in God's name, whatever happens, don't call the police."

Jenkyns smiled wanly. "Aye, I can do that, Miss Nita," he said. "But I hate to think of you putting yourself in the hands of that awful man."

Nita's hand strayed to her gun, and her sweet mouth compressed, became a straight line that was very much like the Spider's own when he battled against odds.

She called the dog, fastened the leash and gave it into Jenkyns' hand. Together they left the building.

A newsboy dashed up as she crossed to the powerful Hispana Suiza.

"Wuxtra!" he shouted in her ear. "Wuxtra! Black Death kills twenty! Spider hunted! Wuxtra!"

Nita almost flinched from the words. The Black Death. It meant a disease to the people, a plague that hung like a pestilential cloud over the city. To her it meant a sinister voice over the wire, a criminal genius who held her lover's life in vicious, tormenting hands.

She flung into the roadster, with the easy competence of experience touched the motor to deep-throated life. A glance at her watch. Fifteen minutes remained of the time the Black Death had allotted!

Her foot was heavy on the accelerator and the droning motor sped her uptown through nearly deserted streets. She parked at Fifty-Seventh and Madison and walked slowly up the avenue.

Behind her she glimpsed the taxi that contained Jenkyns and her faithful dog, but she dared not glance back again lest she arouse suspicions and foredoom her efforts to save Dick.

She heard the purr of auto tires, the metallic opening of a door, and a black sedan stood at the curb with motor running, its rear door open. Within, all was darkness.

WITH AN effort Nita kept her hand away from the gun in her pocket. Her elbow clamped tight against the package of money beneath her arm. The chauffeur sat with his eyes rigidly front, no one else was visible, but a hateful voice that Nita recognized, called softly,

"Your car awaits, Miss van Sloan."

Nita forced her feet to carry her toward that yawning black interior and climbed stiffly in.

Not until then did she glimpse the man who had called. A faint glimmer of light seeped beneath a shade and revealed a large, broad shouldered man. There was no face, but eyes stabbed at her through the slits of a black mask.

The door slammed, and the car slid forward. Nita was very near despair. Of what use was her dog now? Of what use Jenkyns' faithful shadowing?

"Where is Dick?" she demanded. "I won't give you the money until...."

The man's soft laughter checked her words. She knew without explanation the meaning of that ugly mirth. To talk of giving him the money when she was in his power, in the power of a man so fiendish that he had loosed the Plague upon the city!

For a wild moment Nita considered snatching her gun, but even as she hesitated it was too late. The man's hand closed like a metal band about her wrist, took the revolver, then deliberately searched her entire person, for other weapons.

Nita's face burned with humiliation, but her angry protest earned only mocking laughter. One thought buoyed her, the hope that soon she would be with Dick. It might avail no more than that they should die together. But even so she went gladly.

It was fifteen minutes later, after many turnings, that the girl felt the car draw to a stop. The man with the mask held a gun so that she could see its glint and said softly:

"I would advise against any outcry. I would dislike to put a bullet into your lovely body, but I should not hesitate to do so if the necessity arose."

He opened the door and Nita stepped out silently, found herself looking up at an elaborate apartment building.

Her heart beat wildly. Soon now she would see Dick. Sudden fear caught her by the throat. If—if this monster had kept his word and not harmed him.

A man walked on either side of her, and she got no opportunity to discover whether Jenkyns had followed, whether Apollo would be able to help if the need arose.

She was whisked into the building through the basement entrance, up many flights of stairs. The masked man roughly dismissed the chauffeur then, and with fingers clamped about Nita's arm, led her to a door. She heard the key grate. Light smote her eyes.

She started forward, eagerly, but the hand on her arm held her back, and the man's gloating laughter rang in her ears.

"In a hurry, Miss van Sloan? Sorry, but I must detain you a moment." And he held her while they walked slowly down a long hallway and entered a sparsely furnished room.

There Nita halted. A tremulous smile lifted her lips. Dick at last! But not the Dick she had always known. The man before her was plainly helpless—and there was a despairing droop to his shoulders that spoke clearer than words of lost hope....

CHAPTER 10
GREAT APOLLO

WENTWORTH'S WRISTS were handcuffed before him and another shackle about his ankles secured him to a steam pipe. His tool kit had been discovered by the Black Death and lay open upon the floor before him. Men had examined it. Tied to the bed lay Virginia Doeg, her red hair tousled, her face swollen, still in a stupor from the effects of drugs.

Wentworth smiled slowly, deepening the taut lines of his face. His eyes seemed to grow more haggard.

"Darling, darling," he said, "why did you come?"

"Scarcely complimentary to the lady, my dear Mr. Wentworth," jeered the man behind the mask. "I marvel that she finds you so attractive."

Nita tugged against his restraining hand. "Oh, please, please," she said, and, released, ran to Dick and threw her arms about him. For a moment she forgot all the evilness of her surroundings in the joy of being with him again. He buried his face in the softness of her hair, murmuring over and over, "Darling."

But Nita was not entirely absorbed in the greeting, happy as she was to be with Dick again. Her mind was working swiftly, seeking some way to help him escape. She put little credence in this man's promise to let her ransom Wentworth. But she turned to him with seeming confidence.

"Now turn him loose," she said, smiling. "You have the money."

The man regarded her steadily through the slits of his mask and made no answer. Nita walked toward him, her eyes pleading, her hands half outstretched.

"I have fulfilled my part of the bargain," she said. "It is your turn to do as you promised."

She was quite close to him now. The beginnings of laughter shook him. He chuckled in amusement, threw back his head, and, like an uncoiling spring, Nita leaped forward, snatched for the gun she had seen him place in his pocket. The man snapped his arms about her. They were like steel bands and she was

And now, Ram Singh burst into the room—knife gleaming in right hand—drawn back to throw.

helpless. He laughed at her struggles, lifted her bodily from the floor and carried her well away from Wentworth.

"Almost caught me napping," he chuckled. "Ah, but I admire a brave and pretty woman." He took her hat from her head and

ran his hand through her tangled curls, tilted up her face. He laughed again. "Only the necessity for wearing my mask," he said, "prevents me paying proper tribute to your beauty."

He turned toward the Spider, straining futilely against his

shackles. "Perhaps," the masked man went on softly, "when we have disposed of your—friend…."

WENTWORTH FORCED himself to calmness. Showing agitation would merely be fuel to the flames of this man's love of torture. He laughed shortly.

"A petty criminal to the last," he jeered, "pulling petty little tricks. The Black Death? You haven't the brain to conceive such a thing."

Holding Nita helpless, the man turned the blank face of his mask to Wentworth.

"And the Spider gives evidence of human emotion," he mocked. "Imagine the Spider, the great altruist, being swayed by mere jealousy!"

Wentworth's face was disdainful, and in his eyes Nita caught a gleam that gave her hope. But it was only for a moment. Dick was courageous beyond all men she knew, but bravery could not break those gleaming shackles of steel that held him prisoner.

"Just a muscle-man," the Spider jeered, "a fool sleeping in the King's bed, pretending to be the Black Death. Why you—"

And the masked man laughed!

"Give up, Spider," he said. "I'll admit you're clever. But when you try to goad me into talking, you're merely amusing. You've been trying now for two hours, excepting for the twenty minutes it took to collect your girl friend, and you've learned precisely nothing."

It was the Spider's turn to laugh. The two men glared at each other fiercely.

"You think so?" Wentworth sneered.

Nita remained quiescent in the man's grasp. She could feel his anger mounting in the tightening grip of his fingers on her arms. They bit like the pinchers of the Inquisition, but she made no sound. Dick seemed to be trying to infuriate the man. If he would forget her for an instant, she might strike him from behind! She felt his fingers loosen, and relaxed her muscles for the test. A chuckle trickled from behind the mask. The steel fingers thrust Nita toward the bed, held her while he tied her.

"Yes, you are clever, Spider," the man said, "but not quite clever enough. It is a pity—"

He crouched and snarled suddenly, whirling toward Wentworth, helpless in his shackles of steel—"a pity you must die."

SLOWLY, WHILE Nita watched with horror-widened eyes, he drew from his pocket the automatic she had tried to snatch.

"You were right, Wentworth," he said. "I only wanted the girl here so I could kill her with you. There was just the slightest chance that you might have struck some trail that pointed to me and confided your suspicions to her.

"But—" the gloating laughter cackled out, "—the Black Death leaves only dead behind. There will be no tales told."

He raised his gun.

"No, no!" Nita said, "No, not that! I'll do anything, anything, but please!"

The masked man did not even turn his head. The softness was gone from his voice now and it grated harshly like rusty iron.

"You are hardly in a position, my dear, to make promises. It is I who shall dictate, you who shall obey. But first—"

The gun snapped up. Wentworth dropped to the floor as lead whined past. He seized the shackle about his ankle, and it came loose in his hand!

He sprang toward his enemy. But in mid leap he checked and twisted aside. Behind him, he heard the snarl of an animal raging.

The curtains before the window were whipped aside and a tawny shape hurtled across the room straight at the throat of the Black Death!

Wentworth rolled aside, shouting, "Get him, Apollo!" and Nita jerked to her feet, shouting excited encouragement to the great dog. But the masked man whirled like a flash, and the upswung movement of his gun and the crash of its explosion were almost simultaneous.

Apollo's leap sent him crashing against the man's chest, sent the crook reeling backward across the room with arms waving frantically to recover his balance. But Apollo, great Apollo, plunged to the floor and lay quivering, helpless to move a muscle of his powerful body.

The Black Death brought up heavily against the wall, partly dazed. His gun came up slowly.

And now Ram Singh burst into the room, knife gleaming in his right hand, drawn back to throw. For a single instant the masked man wavered, then turned and fled.

Ram Singh's hand flashed forward, the knife glittered in the air. The door clapped shut, and the blade ground its point upon that metal barrier, and crashed futilely to the floor.

"A gun. Ram Singh!" Wentworth cried sharply.

The Hindu caught one from his pocket and tossed it to him. Miraculously Wentworth's hands were free of the shackles, and he caught the weapon, raced across the room and snatched open the door.

CHAPTER 11
VIRGINIA'S CLUE

GUN FLAME lanced at Wentworth. His answering shot was lightning fast and drew a curse of pain.

"The lights, Ram Singh," he shouted.

Darkness shut down like a lid. Gun din filled the hall, and lead chunked into the door at the Spider's elbow. Suddenly then he groaned aloud, threw himself noisily to the floor and rolled silently toward the gunman.

He heard muttered obscenity:

"Got the damned idiot!"

Wentworth grinned thinly and fired upward at the voice. A scream began and choked. A body slammed against the wall, slithered to the floor. The Spider rose. The pencil beam of his flash showed the broken-nosed man, shot through the mouth, dead.

The Black Death had fled, leaving his henchman to kill his foe!

Wentworth padded swiftly down stairs, then checked sharply,

a curse of disappointment on his lips. Police whistles! Either the Black Death had given the alarm, or the shots had been heard.

Wentworth smiled and raced upward, almost slammed into Ram Singh coming down.

"Quick!" he snapped. "The police. Carry Apollo!"

He darted into the apartment where he had been held prisoner. Apollo stood on trembling legs in the middle of the floor, a bloody tear across his skull. Seeing Wentworth, he tried feebly to wag his tail.

"Stout fellah!" cried Wentworth, "Good dog!"

He clapped the dog on the back, snatched out a knife and freed Nita and Virginia Doeg. He shook the drugged girl, fought to rouse her from her stupor. While they worked Nita asked swift questions.

"How in the world, Dick," she demanded, "did you get those handcuffs off? How did Ram Singh find you and—"

Dick smiled grimly as he worked. "It's all your doing, darling," he said.

"But, I—"

"Shhh," the Spider silenced her. "You did it. I let drop a hint to the Black Death that you knew as much as I did about this business, and you did the rest. He called you up, and I pretended to be worried. Then, when he left to meet you, I used a file I had hidden in these shoes—" he pointed to the thick, soft rubber soles—"when I knew I had to walk into his trap. But the filing took so long that the Black Death's car was at the door before I was free. I just had time to phone Ram Singh—

whom I had told to await my call near here—and to put the cuffs back on, when you entered. I was hoping to capture him. And I put off the showdown as long as possible, trying to learn something about his plans. But even when he thought he was going to kill me certainly, he was too cautious to talk."

He straightened and gazed down at the still stupefied Doeg girl.

"No use working on her any more," he said. "She can walk if she's led."

He turned toward Ram Singh and found the Hindu crouched behind the metal door. He spun toward the door, but found no danger threatening there. Frowning, he puzzled over Ram Singh's apparent fright.

THEN HE realized for the first time that Ram Singh was not wearing his turban, that his close-shaved head was bald! That, to a Hindu, was shameful. The Spider found his own hat and gave it to Ram Singh, being careful to hide the laughter that lurked behind his eyes.

"How is it," he asked in Hindustani when Nita, leading Virginia Doeg had started toward the door, "that thou hast lost thy turban, Ram Singh?"

The man answered with extreme dignity in the same language. "Oh *Sahib,* it was in thy service. I feared to enter by the door lest the noise of it should cause thy captor to shoot. So disgraced one that I am, I used my turban to lower that unclean beast whom thou callest Apollo to the fire escape so that he might avert the tragedy which threatened here. That is why it was that beast which was first to enter the room and not thy servant, Ram Singh."

Wentworth placed his hand upon his man's shoulder. "Verily, oh Ram Singh," he said, "thou art a man, and through all India it shall be sung how Ram Singh bared his head that he might save his master."

Pride gleamed in Ram Singh's eyes and he stood no longer ashamed.

The sirens of police radio cars echoed in the streets now. There was need to hurry. Wentworth caught up the body of the man he had slain and, with it over his shoulder, led the way swiftly downward until they reached the first floor.

They heard then the shouts of policemen, the battering of axes on the door below. Wentworth laid the body of the man at the head of the steps, gun in hand. Then, smiling grimly, he affixed the seal of the Spider upon his forehead.

"That will stop them a while," he murmured to Nita. Quickly he unlocked an apartment, and sped to a window which opened on the back.

Suddenly Nita quit the other girl and grasped his arm.

"The cigarette lighter, Dick, the one that man planted on you. Throw it away!"

Wentworth laughed softly as he raised the window.

"A souvenir of the Black Death!" he whispered. "I wouldn't lose it for the world!"

"But—" the girl started to protest.

The Spider kissed her swiftly on the lips, smothering the words, helped her over the sill and lowered her by her hands to the ground. It was a drop of only a few feet. Rapidly he lowered the others after her. Then he and the great dog sprang down themselves.

The Spider and those with him faded into the shadows.

THE RISING sun was red in the sky as Wentworth and his tired company threaded the city. But even at this early hour the streets resounded with the shouts of newsboys, crying the toll of the Black Death. A hundred killed!

Wentworth's jaws locked. A hundred dead! The Black Death was striking more savagely. While Wentworth battled futilely against his traps, sought frantically for some clue to the man's identity, the black wings of the Plague were sweeping the city, as its purple flower of pain blossomed on scores of throats.

But Wentworth had the girl, Virginia Doeg, at least. When she had thrown off the drugs, he would question her. Desperately he hoped for a clue from her.

Later, when she had slept off the narcotic, safe in his apartment with Nita, he went to the girl.

Though his eyes were grim with the thought of the ravages of the Black Death ever at the back of his mind, he was gentle with Virginia Doeg as he insisted upon her answering the question that he had put to her a few hours ago. A smile twisted his lips—it seemed like years.

When last he had asked that question, fear had gleamed for a moment in her eyes. Then a man with a gun had interrupted their conversation. It was that fear which had led the Spider to believe that she might hold some clue to the identity of the Black Death.

"Who besides yourself," he asked again, "had the opportunity to substitute the forged bonds for the genuine?"

And once more the girl evaded his keenly questioning gaze. Wentworth frowned. "Surely now," he said, "you must realize the importance of answering that question. Your failure to answer it was the reason for all that has happened. Your kidnapping by that masked man."

"Oh," she shuddered, "that horrible Spider."

Bewilderment clouded Wentworth's eyes. His sharp glance flicked to Nita, and he saw a sly smile about her mouth.

Then suddenly he understood. Nita had convinced the girl, whose drug-dazed memories were befuddled, that the man who had kidnapped her was the Spider.

Wentworth had believed it necessary to reveal to this girl that the Spider and Wentworth were one. And now Nita cleverly had kept the secret. His eyes gave her silent thanks, as he picked up the thread of thought that the girl's cry of revulsion had revealed.

"Unless you want the Spider to come again," he said sternly, "you had better answer my question at once."

THE FRIGHTENED girl looked up at him, large-eyed and pale, beneath the glowing red shower of her hair. "Oh," she said, "he couldn't have done it. Not my Jimmy!"

"Jimmy?"

The girl spoke rapidly now. "Yes, Jimmy. He could have done it, but I know he didn't. He loves me. We are to be married. And he is not the only one. Any official of the firm could have done it."

"What's Jimmy's name?" Wentworth said softly.

"But he isn't guilty," the girl protested. "I know he isn't."

"Of course not," the Spider reassured her, "but I would like to know the name of—" he smiled—"the lucky man."

Virginia Doeg blushed, and dropped her eyes. "Jimmy Handley," she said.

"Ah, yes," said Wentworth, remembering then MacDonald Pugh's mention of the man. An intelligent youth, Pugh had said, one who was "going places." Was it possible that the girl was Handley's dupe, that he had substituted the forged bonds and given the germs to her dog, so that when the time came he could direct suspicion upon her by claiming that the bonds had been stolen to finance the start of this monstrous crime?

Wentworth nodded swiftly to Nita, signifying that the girl could go now, and left the room hurriedly. He glanced at his watch. It was late, nearly four o'clock.

He caught his hat and cane from Jenkyns' ready hand, strode into the hall, and a moment later a taxi was whisking him through the late afternoon traffic to the offices of Pugh & Works, Inc., on Wall Street.

Straight down Broadway they whirled until that famous thoroughfare became a narrow street that belied its name, until the graveyard that marked one end of Wall Street hove into view, and they whirled into the narrow canyon that was the money center of the world.

The taxi jerked to a halt. Wentworth tossed the driver a bill and climbed out. A two-seated green Ford with P.D. printed on its side, a radio patrol car of the police, was parked ahead of him.

The devil! Was he going to run into some new crime at every turn of the trail that the Black Death left? He told himself that he was foolish, that the police car had no connection with his errand. But when he thrust into the elaborate offices of the brokerage firm of Pugh & Works, he found the two policemen from the patrol car there before him.

And MacDonald Pugh himself, his high shoulders stooped, his forward-leaning bald head nodding emphasis to his words, was talking to them.

Wentworth caught the tag end of what he was saying. "There is no doubt about it," Pugh was declaring positively. "There is a shortage in his accounts. He left the office early yesterday and he has not returned."

"And what's his name, sir," one of the officers demanded.

MacDonald Pugh looked up with dark eyes from beneath his almost white brows, saw Wentworth and raised a hand in affable salute. "Just a minute, Dick," he said, and turned back to the policeman.

"The man's name," he said, "is James Handley."

CHAPTER 12
WENTWORTH VIEWS THE PLAGUE

JAMES HANDLEY, the man Virginia had said could not be guilty! The man she was to marry! There was a shortage in his accounts—and he was missing!

Wentworth was keenly interested. But no hint of it showed in his face. He flicked ashes from his cigarette and lounged about the office, inspecting the oil paintings which hung upon its walls as if totally disinterested in the conversation between Pugh and the two policemen.

But the name apparently had been dismissal for the two officers. "We'll put out an alarm for him, sir," one of them told Pugh. "And you may depend, sir, that we'll pick him up very shortly. They can't escape our dragnet."

"Fine," said MacDonald Pugh heartily, and the policemen left.

"Good of you to call, Dick," Pugh said to him, and Wentworth turned smiling from the inspection of a portrait.

"You have atrocious taste in paintings, Mac," he said, "but you have managed to get one good piece here. Undoubtedly a Millet."

MacDonald Pugh smiled. "You didn't come here, Dick, to criticize my paintings, I'm sure."

"No," Wentworth told him. "I was down this way, thought of you, and recalled that promise of a fishing party some weekend.

The tuna are running off Montauk, you know. A bit early, but I understand some large ones have been taken."

"That's damned nice of you," Pugh said. "But I don't see how I could possibly get away. The stock market is doing tricks these days, what with the NRA and Mr. Roosevelt's so-called controlled inflation."

Wentworth waved a hand negligently, tossing his cigarette into a smoking stand. "You business men," he sighed. "I wish I could find something in life that was half so interesting. Sure you can't make it, Mac?"

Pugh shook his bald head regretfully, smiling up from beneath those white brows. "No can do. But if you're out at your estate over Sunday, and decide finally not to go fishing, you might drop over. Bring Nita along. When the ticker stops Saturday noon, I have until the Stock Exchange opens Monday before I—"

A strangled cry rang through the office.

Wentworth whirled, staring with narrowed eyes past Pugh to the door of an office marked "Private." The door swung haltingly open and a man staggered out, clutching at his throat.

"The Black Death!" he gasped. "I've got it!"

His hand ripped his collar open, and on the corpse-like yellowness of his throat Wentworth saw the purple flower of the dread plague!

The man was Theodore Works, Pugh's partner, and there could be no doubt that he was dying. His stumbling entry had thrown the room into a panic. Stenographers sprang screaming from their tasks, and pale-faced men raced in panic for the street.

Even Pugh, with one terrified glance, joined in the pell-mell rush. And only Wentworth, jaw clenched and eyes aglint, remained.

THE MAN collapsed into a seat, flung his arms across a desk top and leaned his chest against its edge, his breath coming hoarsely.

"You have been blackmailed?" Wentworth demanded.

The man stared at him unseeingly. Wentworth moved a step nearer and demanded again, "Were you blackmailed?"

This time the man's head nodded heavily. "Yes. And I paid."

His hoarse voice was scarcely human, the words mere mouthings. "I paid. And now—oh, God—I'm dying anyhow! Dying—the Black Plague—"

"Whom did you pay?" Wentworth snapped at him. Sympathy for the dying man touched him, but more than sympathy was at stake. Here was a man who had actually had contact with the dread master of the plague, had paid him blackmail. If he could obtain from him with his dying breath a clue that might save the countless millions of the city—

Works' head sagged forward. Breath rasped more harshly in his throat. He belched. Blood poured from his jaws. It tore a muffled scream of agony from him.

"Quick, man!" Wentworth shot at him. "Do you know who the blackmailer was?"

The sagging head raised an Inch, wobbled slowly in negation.

"No—" Works got out, "but—voice on wire—thought I knew it."

Wentworth advanced two swift strides. Here was the Black Death in all its horror. Its contagion might strike him down. But here, too, might be the one clue that the Spider must have to track the plague master.

Suddenly Works convulsed, reared back in his chair with clutching hands digging into his throat.

"Speak, man, speak!" Wentworth cried.

The purple lips opened, suffocation blackened his face. Blood gushed out. Sound issued from that ghastly mouth. But it was sound that was translatable into no word. It was the death rattle. And Works slumped forward upon the desk, his face dyed by the loathsome blush of the Black Death.

For an instant longer Wentworth stared at the body, his heart torn with compassion at the cruelty he had been forced to exert upon this dying man. Then he whirled and strode from the room with hard-pounding heels.

Gone was the airy nonchalance with which he had met MacDonald Pugh; gone the smile from his lips, and in its place was grim purpose.

From his path a man fled, running with a wobbling unaccustomed gait, a sloppy unpressed coat flapping in the wind, a dilapidated gray felt jammed down about his ears.

For an instant Wentworth pursued. But after two swift strides he checked himself. A grim twist that was only half a smile came to his lips.

He should know by now the earmarks of the gentlemen of

the press, should know that no one but a careless, keen reporter would dare, as this man had, the curse of the Black Death for the comparatively trivial accomplishment of spreading first the news of a major story upon the front page of his paper.

Wentworth strode on to the curb and hailed a taxi, cried sharply, "Police headquarters!" Then he settled back upon the cushions and toyed with the head of his cane, looking down at its carved ivory handle with eyes that for once were unappreciative of its artistry.

It was time the news was spread abroad, time that the city learned that this Black Death was the work of a human agency. Then indeed would the whole world rise up to wipe out the sinister masked shadow that crouched with bloody hands over New York's millions.

BUT BEFORE his cab could traverse the mile between Wall Street and the headquarters of police, men were screaming extras on the streets, and black headlines blazoned forth the news that the Black Death was a blackmailer's plot.

Perhaps, Wentworth thought, that news would help bring in information from others that had been blackmailed; perhaps it would bring out a clue to the plague master himself. But though he doubted that the police would be able to find the man, there was a way in which they could help if they would. They could, in all probability, locate James Handley. If they would search in earnest for that man, putting their best men upon the case, it was at least possible that some definite lead might be uncovered.

But Wentworth entered the office of the Commissioner with

a feeling of futility. How could he convince Kirkpatrick of the necessity for that search, unless he revealed not only what Wentworth knew, but what the Spider had learned?

Kirkpatrick's face brought Wentworth to a stop just inside the door. It was the face of a living man who was dead, the face of a man haunted by a tragic fear, or tortured by a secret grief. He stared at Wentworth with eyes that were unblinking and utterly cold, deep-sunk beneath frowning brows. And for once, his mustache was untidy and unpointed, and his clothes, usually immaculate, were unpressed.

"Why do you come here?" he demanded harshly.

Wentworth stared at him without speech, and once more the Commissioner rasped:

"Why do you come here?"

Wentworth was unprepared for the attack. His lips moved stiffly in a smile that was without mirth. "I came to help—"

"I don't want your help," thundered Kirkpatrick. He smacked his fist on the desk and crouched over it like a man about to spring. His eyes were burning.

"In heaven's name, Stanley, what is the matter with you?" Wentworth demanded.

There was a sternness in his face and his eyes did not waver before the assault of Kirkpatrick's glare. For two full minutes the men stared so into each other's eyes, and then Kirkpatrick straightened slowly from his tense crouch, dragged a heavy hand across his furrowed brow.

He sank limply back into his chair, and Wentworth came forward until he stood just across the desk from the Commissioner. He was smiling easily now, and offered his cigarette case to Kirkpatrick.

"You gave me quite a start, Stan," he said. "You must be under a terrific strain."

Kirkpatrick made no move to accept the proffered cigarette. He seemed infinitely tired, sagging in his seat like a man almost without life. But his hands upon the arms of the chair were white with the tension of his gripping fingers.

"Wentworth," he said slowly, in a voice that was as dull and empty as his eyes. "I have long suspected that you were the Spider. I have had no proof of it. God knows I didn't want proof of it, except as my duty drove me on. For the Spider to me was an admirable man, despite his crimes against the law. He struck down criminals that I could not touch because of the rigid regulations of that law. And he avenged the innocent. For that I revered him, respected him as I respected you."

Wentworth opened his mouth to speak, but Kirkpatrick's eyes stopped him. "I say respected," he went on, "but that is past now. And I'm warning you that any other Commissioner of Police, knowing what I know, would believe the Spider, believe *you,* guilty of the Black Death!"

Kirkpatrick stopped speaking and his chin sagged upon his chest. But still his burning eyes held those of his friend. He leaned toward him across the desk.

"This is—" Wentworth began. But once more the Commissioner stopped him, this time with a tired lift of his hand.

"Knowing you, Wentworth," he said, "knowing the Spider of days past, I cannot believe a man of those humanitarian instincts could inflict the Black Death upon the city.... If I did believe you capable of that—" Suddenly the Commissioner snapped to his feet, stood rigidly, his fists clenched tightly at his sides. "If I believed that Wentworth, *I'd shoot you down this minute in cold blood!*"

CHAPTER 13
A SHOT IN THE DARK

KIRKPATRICK'S INTENSITY startled Wentworth for a moment, drove all thoughts of protest from him. The patent distress of his friend touched him.

He tried to smile, failed, tried again, and achieved a stiff travesty of mirth.

"And so you should, Stanley," he said, "shoot me down if I were the Spider—and if the Spider were guilty of the Black Death."

Kirkpatrick's saturnine face did not lighten. "I think it wise that you go now," he said dully, "and do not return."

"But this is foolish," Wentworth protested. And now for the first time a thin smile lifted Kirkpatrick's lips.

"The foolish part of it," he said, "is that I do not arrest you, as my inspectors urge me to."

An almost perceptible start jerked at Wentworth's muscles. So Kirkpatrick was not alone in his suspicion! This was a thing that he had not realized before. He had thought the whole thing a figment of Kirkpatrick's tortured imagination. This revelation increased the seriousness of the situation.

"For God's sake, go!" Kirkpatrick ground out, and the strain showed in the thinness of his voice. "Can't you understand?"

And now at last Wentworth did understand. He bowed with grave formality. "Very well," he said, turned on his heel and stalked to the door. And even while he was closing it he heard the Commissioner's cracked voice rise madly:

"And—don't—come back!"

The uniformed clerk who stood outside the door stared at Wentworth with narrowed, suspicious eyes. But for once the glance remained unseen. Wentworth's keen senses were dulled by the enormity of the rift between him and his warmest friend.

He could see how Kirkpatrick was torn between duty and affection; between what his office urged and what his heart believed. Even the monstrous threat of the plague paled before this personal grief. It seemed like some nightmarish thing that could not actually exist.

Wentworth dazedly entered a taxi and gave his home address, hoping desperately that Nita would be there. He needed her warm understanding now, needed the consolation of her confidence and belief in him.

The taxi seemed to crawl. He was on fire to get home. He leaned forward and rapped on the glass. "Hurry, man, hurry!" he snapped. "Speed."

Tell a taxi driver to hurry in New York and you get the wildest ride that can be achieved by human ingenuity and mechanical power. Fender-brushing, brake-slamming, tire-squealing speed!

Off slammed the taxi, weaving through traffic like a rabbit running through brambles. It whirled a corner on dry-skidding tires, dodged a head-on collision by a fraction of an inch, spurted between two encroaching trucks.

Wentworth, feverish-eyed, tense-muscled, leaned forward and rapped on the glass. "Faster," he cried, "Faster!"

THE TAXI driver whipped a frightened glance over his shoulder, the whites of his eyes showing, and suddenly Wentworth laughed. The man must think him utterly mad.

But the driver was trying desperately to fulfill the demand of this grim-faced passenger behind him, for when a passenger asks favors it means big tips. And even in taxi-riding New York big tips are scarce nowadays.

He locked tires and skidded the last twenty-five feet to the curb before Wentworth's apartment house, and the violence of the stop almost flung his passenger forward upon his shoulders. Wentworth dropped to the pavement, tossed the man a twenty-dollar bill and, laughing with a cracked strain in his voice, went pounding into the house.

Behind him the taxi driver looked from the twenty dollar bill to his retreating back, shook his head and muttered, "Jeez, the guy's nuts!"

Wentworth slammed into the elevator, and its express speed seemed infinitely slow. Key in the lock, he thrust open the door violently, strode into the center of the drawing room before he paused and stood stock still, staring about him. Nita wasn't there.

Wentworth's broad shoulders slumped. Jenkyns' staid old figure plodded into the room, took his master's hat and cane from listless hands. Twice he opened his mouth to speak, and twice thought better of it. Finally he turned and plodded out again, his white old head shaking.

Wentworth moved on stumbling feet into the music room beyond, his fumbling hands brought out his violin case, picked up the instrument and thumbed slowly over the resonant strings. Their notes rang sweet and true, and he tucked the violin beneath his chin, touched bow to the strings.

Dirge-like the music rolled, funereal and slow. But as he played new animation seemed to come into his drooping figure, his fingers flicked more rapidly over the strings, his bow surged—and the music's tempo changed, became furious and wild.

It was mad, that music, as if all the devils of hell leaped in those flicking fingers. Jenkyns' frightened face showed in the doorway. He knew his master's habit of playing out his moods, but never before had he heard such wild notes torn from the straining strings.

The music spoke of a mind on the verge—the verge of....

Ram Singh appeared behind him, his dark face like carven stone with eyes glittering to the pulse of the music. But Wentworth was utterly unaware of the two faithful servitors at his back. All his being was centered on the vibrating instrument beneath his chin.

Gradually the wildness died, and in its place came a slow, limpid melody. But it was two hours after he had picked up the violin that he replaced it in its case and, exhausted, weary in every fiber, turned to find Ram Singh and Jenkyns standing transfixed in the doorway.

He smiled at them quickly. "My dinner clothes, Ram Singh.

Jenkyns, phone Miss Nita that I shall call for her in half an hour."

"Yes, sir!" Jenkyns bobbed with bows, his ruddy face wreathed in smiles, and ducked away as fast as his old legs would carry him to perform his master's will....

NITA AND Wentworth went forth gaily to dinner. And not until the meal was well under way did he mention, and then only casually, the afternoon scene with Kirkpatrick. He was callous about it, as if the friendship lost meant less than nothing, and Nita's quick blue eyes went to his face and searched it carefully.

She was a lovely girl, and in evening dress she was surprisingly beautiful. The low-cut gown of simple white left bare the exquisite slope of her shoulders. The gleam of her rich brown hair made a jewel-like setting for the perfect oval of her face.

The luxurious dining room was muted by the depression, its usually crowded tables half empty, but not a man who passed but felt his pulses swiften, felt the dread curse of the plague lift a little for having glimpsed her and paid the tribute of admiring eyes.

But her gaze was solely upon Wentworth. Her eyes hovered now half between puzzlement and raillery. Well as she knew her Dick, she did not quite understand this new mood.

"But this is silly, Dick," she said.

Wentworth leaned forward across the spotless white and crystal of the table. "You have the dearest chin in the world," he said.

"Be serious, Dick," she urged.

"Oh, I really mean it," he said.

She placed her small white hand upon his. "Dick, you're maddening sometimes," she said. "Tell me about this spat you had with Kirkpatrick."

"Spat?" Wentworth's eyebrows lifted, the hint of raillery that always lurked there emphasized. He laughed. He placed his other hand upon hers and leaned forward again. "Nita," he said, "I'm bored with the city. I think I shall go to the country for the weekend."

The girl looked at him with a faint frown disturbing her forehead. She did not speak.

"We have an invitation," he went on, "from MacDonald Pugh. A charming fellow, don't you think? And this constant business of the Black Death, this pursuit of shadows, grows irksome."

"Stop fooling, Dick," the girl pleaded, the frown deepening between her eyes. She smiled uncertainly. "What's the matter, boy?"

"I'm bored," he repeated.

She was completely serious now. "What are you trying to do?" she asked in level tones. "This isn't like you, Dick."

Wentworth's smile was crooked. "Can't I pick a quarrel with my only sweetheart?" he demanded.

"What are you up to, Dick?" she demanded again.

"Just this," he said in swift undertones. "I want everyone to believe that I have left the city. I wanted you to believe it too. You are too honest, too lovely to be able to dissemble successfully. And everyone—absolutely everyone—must think that I have left."

"And so you tried to pick a quarrel with me?" the girl asked softly, reproachfully.

Wentworth's eyes kissed her.

"It was foolish, darling," he said, and abruptly his face went serious again. "Now, beautiful, get angry with me. Make a scene. Stand up and call me a coward. Say you don't see how I can leave the city when Kirkpatrick needs every man he has, and many more than he has, to track down the Black Death. Go on!"

"Is it really necessary?" the girl asked.

Wentworth's nod was slow and completely serious.

"Very well," she mocked him, "but remember, I am too honest, too lovely, to be able to dissemble!"

SHE SLAPPED her hand upon the table and her blue eyes suddenly clouded. "I don't believe it," she said, and her tones were loud. Dick mumbled some words in a low voice.

Nita's tones rose even higher. "You couldn't do such a thing, Dick Wentworth," she said.

Faces turned at other tables. Startled eyes watched them. "You can't leave the city," she said vehemently in the same loud tone. "You can't. Commissioner Kirkpatrick is your friend. You can't desert him in his greatest need."

Wentworth leaned across the table as if urging her to speak in a lower tone of voice. Audibly he said, "For God's sake, Nita, don't make a scene." But under his breath he whispered, "You're doing splendidly! Keep it up."

Now the girl's voice turned pleading. "But Dick, you must stay, and help Kirkpatrick catch the man behind this dreadful plague. Surely," she jeered at him now, "surely you are not afraid of the Black Death."

Absolute silence fell over the dining-room Her words "the Black Death" rang out stridently. They seemed to strike the room to silent terror. Not a person stirred. The girl was on her feet now, her chair thrust back so violently that it slammed to the floor.

Wentworth was on his feet too. He moved around the table with imploring hands.

"Don't touch me, you coward!" Nita cried. She looked him contemptuously up and down. "To think that Dick Wentworth is a coward!"

She stooped and snatched her fur-edged cloak from the floor, flung it over her arm and half ran, half stumbled down the aisle among the crowded tables, among the staring faces, among the jabbering gossip, her face buried on her forearm as if she were too broken by tears to watch where she went. And as she went she heard the murmured names:

"Dick Wentworth—Nita van Sloan. Dick Wentworth—Nita van Sloan—Nita van Sloan—"

At his table, Wentworth stared like a stricken man after the girl's retreating figure, then sank into his chair, head hanging, one arm sprawled across the table.

FOR LONG minutes Wentworth sat staring fixedly at the table cloth. He too heard the excited jabbering about him, and behind his masking lids his eyes were amused. Mentally he cried, "Brava!" And I said she couldn't act, he thought. Be damned if I don't write a play for her—and he laughed at the conceit. As if Nita would ever desert her aristocratic solitude for the public spotlight of the stage!

Wentworth himself was no mean actor. When he got up from the table he was a grief-crazed man. His stumbling feet found no even path, and his head hung, and his shoulders drooped. But once in the street, away from curious eyes, his alertness returned.

He strode briskly along. Swiftly he returned to his apartment, donned the Spider's dark tweeds, drew a black fedora down over his eyes, and with tool kit beneath his arm, automatic beneath his hand in his pocket, slipped out the servant's entrance and left by the servant's automatic elevator.

The Spider had work to do....

He rode the subway to Wall Street, and the Spider was but another moving shadow among shadows as he slipped into the building where Pugh & Works had offices. The watchman nodded in his chair, and so silent was the invader's tread, so inconspicuous his passage, that even had the man been awake he scarcely would have noticed.

Swiftly then the Spider stole up the stairway, picked the lock of the office door, and fastening it behind him, hurried into the private office of the partners, smelling strongly of disinfectant, and germicides which had been spread to wipe out the threat of the Black Death in the room where Works had died.

The modern safe there resisted his skilled fingers and sensitive ear scarcely longer than had the old tin box in the pawnbroker's office. And in a few moments he had spread before him the firm's books, was skimming rapidly over double-entry bookkeeping and an auditor's report with the skilled ease of a practiced accountant.

His concentration was intense. So engrossed did he become in the frail thread that he followed, the key which involving Jimmy Handley, might bring him to the identity of the Black Death, that he did not hear the opening of the outer door, did not look up until lights flashed on in the main office.

Like a flash then he extinguished his own minute gleaming flashlight by which he had examined the work. Like a shadow he moved across the room, crouched behind a door. And now a black mask concealed his features.

Slow and ponderous footsteps crossed the floor. A hand touched the knob and the door swung open, concealing Wentworth behind it. But the door had been thrust strongly; it struck Wentworth's feet, and, shaking, bounded back. The indistinct figure in the doorway whirled suddenly in alarm. A hand darted up, and at almost point blank range a pistol spurted its spear of powder flame at the crouching Spider!

CHAPTER 14
WHOLESALE DEATH

ONLY WENTWORTH'S split-second coordination of mind and muscle saved him then. He had seen the jerk of the man's hand and thrown himself to the floor so nearly in timing with the gun's discharge that it seemed he had been hurled there by the bullet.

He let the breath hiss from lungs in a half moan, and the crouching figure of the man who had fired straightened slowly. Wentworth's own gun was ready to his hand, but this was no battle with the underworld. In this case he was the interloper; the other man was in the right.

And the Spider never killed an innocent person.

On the other hand, in addition to Pugh, he knew a number of other members of the firm personally, and to be discovered in his present role with a black mask over his face, would have spelled his doom.

He moaned again, his left hand pressed to his chest as if it covered a wound, and abruptly a white light glared into his masked face. The man with the gun moved cautiously nearer. Wentworth tossed on the floor as if in mortal pain, flung out his right arm convulsively.

The man came a step closer, gun ready, and Wentworth's outflung hand found his heel and jerked suddenly. The flashlight flung upward. The man cursed, fell heavily, and his gun blazed.

Glass crashed as a bullet screamed off into the darkness. Wentworth bounded from the floor, flung himself upon the man, and his right fist crashed home twice. The man jerked beneath him, straightened and went limp.

The Spider heard hoarse shouts, the first shrill blasts of a watchman's police whistle. He must make good his escape at once, or it would be too late. Already guards within the building must be rushing to the succor of the man he had knocked out.

Swiftly the Spider ripped out of his coat, flung it and his hat across the room. In them would be found no mark of identification. Swiftly he stooped over the unconscious man, tugged the coat from his body, flapped the other man's hat upon his head, and struggling into the coat, ran toward the outer door, ripping the mask from his face and thrusting it into his pocket as he sped across the room. He jerked open the door, as the first of the watchmen plunged up the stairs, gun up and ready.

The Spider turned his head, staring back over his shoulder at the room he had just left, shouting hoarsely, "In there! He's in there!"

"Jeez, it's you, sir!" cried the watchman. "And I nearly shot you!"

"For God's sake hurry," gasped the Spider hoarsely, and the man plunged past him with drawn gun. Wentworth hastened down the stairs. Behind him, he heard the guard shout a warning to his companions below. "Be careful, Bill. Mr. Robertson is coming down." And in the darkness another guard brushed past him, with a muttered, "Pardon me, sir."

The Spider continued his dash to the front doors. But once there he cut his speed to a quiet stroll, left the building and walked briskly, but with no appearance of flight, through streets that shrieked now with the bedlam of approaching police sirens.

A SUBWAY entrance was near, and Wentworth descended unhurriedly, dropped a nickel into the clanking turnstile and walked slowly up the platform. A bum without hat or coat was stretched out sleeping heavily upon a bench. Grim humor twitched Wentworth's lips. What an evil trick he could play this derelict by the gift of a hat and coat!

He strode into the men's washroom and with powerful fingers shredded the coat he wore. With a knife blade he ripped the hat to fragments and flushed them into the sewer of the city.

After them he sent tie and collar, and slouched again out onto the platform with rumpled hair, a dissolute, half-starved bum. He smeared dirt from the platform upon his cheeks, beneath his eyes, so that they seemed sunken; rubbed his eyes violently so that they became bloodshot. And then it was that his genius for disguise became apparent.

The Spider was gone. Gone, too, was Richard Wentworth, the wealthy young clubman; and in their place, slack-jawed and slouch-shouldered, there lolled upon the bench beside that other slumbering bum, another member of the vast army of the unemployed.

But before police could come pounding, searching down the subway stairs, the rumble of a train filled the hot place. Wentworth shambled aboard and slumped into a corner seat, to all appearances a weary, homeless man.

It was with difficulty that he entered his apartment house again, finally managing to slip into the rear entrance when for a moment the watchman walked away.

And in the morning, as if to mock him, the papers blazed forth with a new horror that transcended all previous perpetrations of that monstrous criminal, the Black Death. For the man had sent letters to every newspaper in town, stating demands that the banks of the city lend a billion dollars to the city government in cash. And that huge sum was to be paid to him! The club this super blackmailer held over the cringing multitude was the threat of the plague spread wholesale through the city!

The letter said:

> If the city's millions knew me better, they would realize that I am no man of idle threats. But since it is unfortunately necessary that I conceal my identity, I shall deliver a free sample of my thoroughness. Even as you in the city read these lines, the Black Death will be among you. Oh, nothing to be alarmed about, for today I shall kill only a few hundred of your millions. Take heed, as these hundreds choke and die with the Black Death, that you do not provoke me by unnecessary delay, lest the next blow wipe out thousands.

And even as newsboys shouted the fearsome headlines the plague had lifted its evil head. Ambulances gonged their way through the streets to the Lower East Side area, where the Black Death had chosen first to strike.

And people died in the streets. Thousands fled.

THE NEWS that the Black Death had fulfilled his warning threw the city into complete panic. Its people went absolutely mad with terror. Thousands fled. Trains and roads were jammed. It was like a wartime evacuation.

Wentworth, roaming the fringes of the area where the Black Death had struck, barred from nearer approach by a double ring of police who, with surgical masks upon their faces braved the plague, found the city about him dead. The usually crowded benches of Battery Park at the tip end of Lower Manhattan were deserted. Even the birds of the air seemed to have fled the Black Death. For the flock of pigeons that usually settled before the Custom House was missing.

And Wentworth, plodding through deserted streets, past the closed doors of shops, of business offices, even of restaurants, saw their bodies in the streets. Good God, even the pigeons had fallen prey to the dread plague.

Wentworth did not approach the stilled birds, but went swiftly to a subway, and riding uptown until he reached a newspaper office went in to insert a small ad.

The place was a hive of industry. Boys darted back and forth with bundles of paper under their arms. Trucks roared off with loads of the latest editions, their headlines still wet with ink, for the thousands who, unable to leave the city, remained behind locked doors or crept furtively through the streets with backward flung glances that seemed to fear the Black Death would spring upon them in the guise of a ravening beast.

A business-like young woman took his ad crisply. It read:

> Pigeons for sale. A large number of all varieties, fancy and homing.

And it gave an address on the upper West Side.

Wentworth made sure that the ad would appear that day, then hurried to the subway again, and sped uptown to the address he had given, where a druggist with whom he had dealt kept pigeons as a hobby.

Wentworth strode up the inner stairs to the man's house

above the store, knocked, and when the bewhiskered little man with gold-rimmed glasses far down upon his nose opened the door, spoke swift.

"I want to board with you for a week. Here's fifty dollars in advance," and he thrust out two twenties and a ten-dollar bill.

The man's fingers closed on the money automatically. But he stared from the crisp new notes to Wentworth's entirely serious face in astonishment.

"I don't understand, Mr. Wentworth—you want to take board with me?"

"That's it."

"But I don't understand."

The pale watery eyes were bewildered. Wentworth smiled grimly. "It is not necessary that you should. You have the money. Do you agree?"

The man stared down at the green banknotes. His head wavered slowly from side to side. "I—I guess it's all right," he stammered. "I'll ask mother."

Wentworth heard his voice calling his wife and knew that when the woman saw the money it would be all right.

ALL THAT day Wentworth sat in the small room that had been assigned to him, waiting. Waiting without action while the corpse fires burned on Riker's Island; while ambulances sirened through the streets; and people choked and died with the Black Death.

It was late when he let himself out of the lonely little apartment and hurried home to get a change of linen. He tarried only a few moments, then hurried back. Climbing the stairs, he heard excited voices raised within.

He knocked on the door and found the bewhiskered little druggist striding back and forth, gesticulating with stiffly waving arms. "They're gone!" he cried. "They're all gone—all my lovely pigeons."

Wentworth's eyes narrowed. "Not stolen?" he demanded.

The little man paused in his striding, peered at him above the gold-rimmed glasses far down upon his nose, peered and blinked and suddenly shouted, "You—you stole my pigeons!"

Wentworth cursed silently. Stolen! And he had expected that the Black Death would come and buy them legitimately. "I'm a dumb fool," he said. His hand reached into his pocket. "How much were the pigeons worth?" he asked.

At sight of the money the man ceased his jabbering. "I'm sorry, Mr. Wentworth," he said, his voice quavering, "I was half out of my head. I know you didn't steal the pigeons."

Wentworth said: "But I put the ad into the paper that caused them to be stolen."

He laid a thousand dollars on the table, whirled and strode from the room. He had been gone from the house scarcely half an hour, yet in that time the Black Death had struck. Was it luck? Or was the arch criminal even now upon his trail?

Wentworth flicked a glance over his shoulder. Hell, he was becoming as frightened as the rabbit-like people of the city, terrified by the plague, who ducked in and out of their doorways like hares out of a warren.

A taxi sped him home. He strode across the room to the

phone without even pausing to remove his hat. Swiftly he called every pigeon fancier he knew, and all either had sold out their complete stocks of pigeons or had been robbed.

That clinched it. He dialed police headquarters, asked for Kirkpatrick, but giving his name was told the Commissioner would not speak to him. Anger flared in Wentworth. This was no time for personal animosity. No time for foolish personal considerations. The entire city was in peril.

He left the house, and a cab sped with him to headquarters. He strode in, and policemen who would have objected stepped from his path, overawed by his blazing eyes. He stormed up to the door of the Commissioner, and there the guard stood firm until the sharp voice from within bade the man step aside and let Richard Wentworth enter.

MORE WORN than ever, Commissioner Kirkpatrick crouched behind the desk. He did not speak until the door had closed behind Wentworth.

"I warned you," he said then, "not to come here again.

"But damn it, man, this is important. There is no time for personal considerations," Wentworth rapped out.

Kirkpatrick's face was grim, his lips so compressed that they showed only as a thin white line. When he spoke again, they opened and shut upon his words like slashing knives.

"I have but one question to ask you," he said. "Why did you steal the pigeons from that man?"

Wentworth stared at him. "Are you mad?" he demanded. "Have you been shadowing me?"

Kirkpatrick smiled grimly. "You leave me no choice, Richard. Give me your cigarette lighter."

Wentworth threw back his head and laughed. It was wild laughter.

"Stanley, in heaven's name, be sensible! I tell you I have the clue that will lead to the capture of the master of the plague."

Kirkpatrick had not moved since Wentworth had entered the room. He still crouched behind his desk, uttering words like bullets.

"Will you hand over the lighter, or must I summon help to take it from you forcibly?"

The gaze of the two men met, and locked. And Wentworth shook his head slowly. "If I do that, will you listen to me?"

The smile that just disturbed Kirkpatrick's lips was wintry. His mouth opened a fraction of an inch.

"Perhaps," he said.

Furiously Wentworth snatched the cigarette lighter from his pocket, the lighter that contained even now the damning seal of the Spider and flung it upon Kirkpatrick's desk. Even if it meant his death he was willing that it should be so, if by so doing he could avert the doom that hung over the city.

Kirkpatrick leaned forward. Under the strong, shaded light upon his desk he examined the lighter. But he had done that futilely before. Now he took out a screw driver and systematically took the thing apart. The white scar upon Wentworth's temple throbbed redly. Even though he was determined to sacrifice his life, if need be, to gain the hearing that was necessary to the salvation of the city, the sight of these lean, probing fingers ferreting nearer and nearer to the secret of the lighter sent the blood thrumming through his veins.

HE WAITED tensely, and his breath came more swiftly. His eyes stared with a fearful intensity. Then abruptly, it was over.

The screw driver touched the hidden spring and the base of the lighter came loose in Kirkpatrick's hand. Wearily, with grief in his eyes, the Commissioner looked up at Wentworth. And the seconds that their eyes met brought hope to the Spider. For he knew that each moment their eyes held the red seals were vanishing.

Kirkpatrick's eyes dropped at last to the lighter. He turned it curiously over in his hand, and Wentworth caught his breath as the Commissioner held it under the light and peered into that secret chamber in its base.

Had the shrewd mechanics of the lighter functioned properly? Had the seals disappeared? With throbbing pulses Wentworth waited. Kirkpatrick's face revealed nothing. It was as if made of steel, its lines drawn so taut it seemed no emotion would ever stir them again.

Then slowly Kirkpatrick looked up.

"I am glad, Richard," he said slowly, "that there are no seals of the Spider to add to the damning evidence my men have piled up against you. This secret chamber in the base of your lighter is enough without that."

"Richard," he said, "I hate to do this, but I have no choice. Any other man in my position would have arrested you days ago. I still cannot believe it, but—"

His hand moved heavily to a row of buttons at the end of

his desk, pressed upon one. Behind Wentworth a door opened, and with the sudden feeling of a trapped animal he whirled and stared into the muzzles of two police pistols, held in the brawny hands of two grim-faced officers.

"Richard Wentworth," Kirkpatrick intoned. He might have been a judge in his black robes with a black cap upon his head, pronouncing doom upon a convicted man. Almost Wentworth could imagine he heard the words, "Dead—dead—dead," that would terminate such a sentence.

"Richard Wentworth, I arrest you on suspicion of homicide," he said. "Take him away."

CHAPTER 15
"IS THAT A CONFESSION?"

WENTWORTH WHIRLED back, staring into Stanley Kirkpatrick's wooden face. The man looked like a sleep-walker, his eyes staring straight ahead, as if they were looking into infinity.

Wentworth started forward, and strong hands gripped his arms.

"In God's name, Stanley, hear me first! Hear me—"

"Take him away."

"—hear me, Stanley!"

"Take—him—away—" Kirkpatrick's voice rose to a shriek.

"Stanley, those pigeons—"

"Shut up!" snarled a voice in Wentworth's ear. He was lifted forcibly, dragged backward.

"Stanley!" he cried.

But the doors slammed between them, and a heavy fist thudded against the base of his skull. Lights danced in his brain, his head sagged, and only half conscious he was dragged with feet that thumped on every stair up a long flight of steps. A cell door clanged metallically and Wentworth was flung inside. He tripped, collapsed upon the concrete floor.

Once more the steel rang. Wentworth thrust his body up from the floor, head dangling. "Stanley," he called. "Stanley!" He caught the bars, dragged himself to his feet. "Stanley!" he cried again, and his voice rang down the steel-barred alleys. He beat upon the iron, shouted, but only the echoes answered him.

And from the next cell a man snarled, "Fer cripes sake, dry up and go to sleep."

And another man muttered, "Youse damned dopes give me a pain. Yuh can't take it."

Wentworth took his hands from the bars, clenched them at his sides until the nails bit into the palms, and forced himself to calmness. In some way he must force Stanley Kirkpatrick to listen to him.

Swiftly he stripped off his belt, climbed upon the iron bed that constituted the cell's sole furniture. He fastened one end to the bars, put the loop about his throat, and let himself sag upon it, sustaining his weight with his hands on the bars so that he could still breathe. Then he beat against the steel as if he kicked in his death agony.

The man in the next cell rolled over and cursed, saw the

With a savage wrench he sent it crashing through the rail—hurtling out into space.

dangling body and shrieked. "Hey, the damned dope's killing himself!"

"God Almighty!" another man cried.

The entire cell block suddenly went mad, cursed, screamed, shouted, beat upon the bars, cried out like a menagerie in a blasting thunder storm. Guards came running, and lights flashed into the cells. Wentworth still hung on by his hands, waiting until the light bathed him. Then he released his hold and dangled in the noose.

Now he actually choked. His tongue thrust up in his throat. His eyes seemed to be starting from their sockets. Blood drummed in his ears. The guard cursed, keys rattled and the door swung open. Powerful hands grabbed Wentworth. He felt himself lifted, the noose jerked free, and he slumped to the floor, almost unconscious.

AND NOW Kirkpatrick came striding, long-legged and somber alone the echoing tiles. He came into the cell where Wentworth lay upon his back on the cot.

Kirkpatrick's face was more drawn than ever. His eyes had a haunted look. "In God's name, Dick," he said, "why have you done this thing?"

Wentworth could not speak above a whisper. His throat had been torn by the metal of his belt buckle. "I must talk to you," he articulated. "Those pigeons—"

Abruptly Kirkpatrick straightened above Wentworth's prostrate body. "Carry this man to my office," he ordered harshly. And Wentworth was lifted bodily and borne away through the still clamoring cells.

In Kirkpatrick's office he was allowed to slump into a chair and the Commissioner stood before him, a gaunt skeleton of his former self, with eyes that glared in near madness.

"Outside," he said abruptly, gesturing to the officers who had brought Wentworth into the room.

One of the men ventured a protest.

"Outside!" Kirkpatrick roared, and the men bolted for the door. Kirkpatrick's eyes still had not left Wentworth's. "Now speak," he croaked hoarsely.

"In God's name, Stanley," Wentworth whispered, his words wide-spaced and painful. "In God's name let me out. I'm the only one in the world who can keep this plague from killing every mortal soul in the city."

The Commissioner's face went pale as death.

"Is that—is that—a confession?" he asked, and his voice sank to a whisper that was as rasping, as painful, as Wentworth's own.

Wentworth, slumped in the chair, stared up at him with sick eyes and with mouth twisted awry in a bitter smile.

"Is that a confession?" Kirkpatrick rasped again, and his voice rose. Suddenly his hand darted beneath his coat. A long-barreled revolver gleamed. Wentworth's eyes did not waver, nor did the twisted smile leave his lips. He continued to stare into Kirkpatrick's face.

But the Commissioner made no move to shoot. He reversed the gun, thrust it toward Wentworth.

"Either kill me or kill yourself," he said. "For, God help me, if you are guilty! But how could you be guilty? I can't believe it." He broke off, panting. "If you are guilty," he said again, "I have failed in my duty to the city." And once more he thrust the gun toward Wentworth.

Slowly his prisoner shook his head. "No man can accuse you of that, Stanley." Wentworth's mind was racing swiftly. He realized now that he could not tell Kirkpatrick the information he had; that he dared not tell him what he had discovered, since to the man's now distraught mind it would seem an additional link in the evidence against him. And Wentworth knew he must get free.

True, he had a clue—but it was a clue that no one but himself could follow to its end; that no one but himself could turn into a weapon against the sinister master of the plague. He must take a long chance—one that would involve his own possible death and that of Stanley Kirkpatrick. But that chance alone would give him his liberty; would in the end enable him to save the city. And he knew that no other hand than his could triumph.

Wentworth stared into Kirkpatrick's eyes. "Take me out of here," he said, "and I will lead you and your men to the master of the plague."

KIRKPATRICK SHOOK his head heavily. He turned his back on Wentworth and strode across the room and back again, pressing his temples with his palms, but no words squeezed from his lips.

"The master of the plague," Wentworth whispered, "I'll take you to him!"

Kirkpatrick's hands dropped. His eyes were dull. "The city is under martial law," he said. "Troops patrol the streets. Any person who leaves his house after dark is shot on sight. Mobs howl about the doors to the City Hall, pound at the doors of the banks, demanding that the Black Death's ransom be paid. And you—you confess at least to complicity in these things, and I let you live!"

He raised a clenched, shaking hand above his head.

"It isn't so, Wentworth," his eyes were pleading. "Dick, it isn't so. You're not guilty! I know you're not guilty! You *can't* be. Why, man—"

For moments the men's eyes met, then abruptly Kirkpatrick crossed to his desk and touched a button. A man sprang into the room. Kirkpatrick looked at him as if he were some strange apparition, but presently he got out words:

"Order out my car. Get a squad of men. Take charge of this prisoner and wait for me. If he tries to escape—kill him."

The man saluted. Others entered the room. Obviously they had been listening. They caught up Wentworth, dragged him from the office. Actually he had recovered most of his strength, but he feigned weakness, let the men carry him.

He had lied to Kirkpatrick. He did not know the hiding place of the Black Death. But a reckless smile twisted his lips. All his money on one spin of the wheel. His life was forfeit anyway. He must gamble the lives of these men, the life of his dearest friend, for the salvation of the city.

Surrounded by police, he was roughed out of the building into the Commissioner's car. He was placed on one of the small, collapsible seats in the tonneau with a man on either side, and two more behind. The Commissioner climbed stiffly into the forward seat. He twisted and stared into Wentworth's face.

"Well?" It was a question.

Wentworth apparently was scarcely able to hold himself erect. "Over Brooklyn Bridge," he whispered. "And hurry. In God's name, hurry!"

The car sprang forward, its deep-throated motor roaring. Its siren began to wail, and it ripped through city traffic at forty, fifty, fifty-five miles an hour. Ahead of them police whistles skirled, traffic cops sprang forward to block traffic, and the Commissioner's car slammed through, spun on to Brooklyn Bridge, and wove a rapid way among other, slower moving cars.

Wentworth sagged forward, his arms upon the back of the seat ahead, his head upon his arms. They raced out into the middle of the span. Ahead of them the roadway was clear. Suddenly Wentworth lunged forward, both his hands grasped the right hand side of the steering wheel and with a savage wrench he sent the car crashing through the rail, hurtling out into space, somersaulting to the river far below.

The top ripped off with the force of the plunge, but Wentworth gripped the wheel and hung on.

Then the car struck and plunged beneath the surface of the East River.

In falling they had just missed the stern of a tug. Men shouted on its decks, ropes snaked out, and one by one the Commissioner and all of his men were hauled to safety. They stared out over the roiled waters of the river. Not a head bobbed in the swift current. Not a ripple except the wash of the boat broke the surface.

Wentworth, the Spider, had vanished.

CHAPTER 16
NITA CRIES VENGEANCE

SPIDER ARRESTED FOR PLAGUE.
KILLS SELF IN BRIDGE LEAP

THOSE BLACK headlines screamed at Nita van Sloan when, with the morning sun warm in her face, she walked briskly along the drive with Apollo, joying in the fresh breezes that swept in from over the Hudson.

"Spider Arrested!" A boy shouted. "Extra! Paper!"

With hands that trembled despite her every effort at control, Nita bought one of the smeary papers, gasped at the headlines, skimmed through the story. Her eyes caught on two sentences and she breathed hope deeply through her nostrils.

> Everyone else in the car was saved by the men on the tug, but the Spider was drowned. The body has not been recovered.

The body has not been recovered. Hope. Hope. But why in the name of heaven had Stanley Kirkpatrick ordered the arrest of his friend? Knowing Wentworth innocent as she did, knowing Kirkpatrick's friendship for him, she could not understand how he could have been driven to such a step.

She saw that Kirkpatrick had been plunged into the river

with Wentworth. Surely from him then, she could learn the truth. She flagged a taxi, sat with whitely clasped hands while it twisted into the express highway, which, elevated on stilts, shot motor traffic down the bank of the Hudson. Once she threw back her head and laughed. But it was as if hands closed on her throat and the laughter stopped. Dead? Dick could not be dead. He could not be! He must not be....

Her name won her instant admittance to the office of the Commissioner, and Kirkpatrick, gray-faced and sleepless, rose to greet her. As the door clicked shut behind her, Nita van Sloan stopped in her tracks, staring at this apparition of the man she had known as gay, debonair, perpetually smiling.

Then she hurried forward, and suddenly her lips were tremulous.

"Tell me! Tell me!" she commanded.

The wintry smile that was Kirkpatrick's only mirth these days stirred his lips. But his deep-sunken eyes remained dull, without life.

"I hope," he said slowly, "and it's for your sake as well as his, that he is dead."

THE GIRL fell back a little staggering half pace, her wrist against her mouth smothering the cry that rose there. But suddenly in those words, too, she found hope.

"You don't know!" she cried at him. "You don't know!"

Kirkpatrick drooped into his chair. "No. I don't know." And a gag seemed taken from his mouth. He began to talk as he had not spoken for days, pouring out words. "You don't know the evidence against him, Nita. It was overwhelming." And he recited the long list of circumstances that pointed to Wentworth as the Spider, and to the Spider as the perpetrator of the Black Death. He seemed suddenly obsessed with the necessity for convincing this girl, perhaps of proving to himself, that he had acted rightly.

"And there in the base of his lighter was a secret compartment," he finished. He spread his hands, palms upward. "I ordered his arrest."

"And you—you," the girl's scorn rang in the room,"—you called yourself his friend."

"But, Nita—"

The girl leaned across the desk and her eyes were burning in a dead white face.

"You know that Dick Wentworth could not do the things you accused him of."

Kirkpatrick eyed her shrewdly. "Yet you yourself quarreled with him, and I do not believe it was for the reason that the gossip columns of the newspapers reported. I believe it was because he could not explain...."

Nita laughed wildly.

"We quarreled. Dear Lord, we quarreled! Dick said that if we pretended to, over his leaving town, it would help convince his enemies that he had left. In which case he would be able to help you better to track down the Black Death.... That was what he said!"

The girl paused, her breasts rising and falling, straining against her dress with the quickness of her breath. She went on more slowly. "Yes, that was what he told me, but I see now that his real reason was to protect me. He knew that he was going into terrible danger. Yes, Dick Wentworth did that, and you think that such a man could—"

Kirkpatrick jerked to his feet. His voice rose and cracked.

"Don't you suppose I know what kind of man Dick Wentworth is? Why do you suppose—"

He stretched out both his hands and they were trembling. "It was the pigeons that clinched the case against him. Whether I believed or not did not matter. I was forced to act."

"The pigeons?"

"Dick offered to take us to the place where the plague master was hidden, where he had concealed the pigeons that, Dick says, bring the plague of the Black Death to the city."

Nita straightened slowly. Pigeons. She shook her head slowly, and all at once she was weary. Her head throbbed. She pressed the back of her hand to her forehead, and the Great Dane pressed against her legs to comfort her.

"Nita—" Kirkpatrick began, moving about the desk.

But the girl shook her head. "No! No!" she cried, and turned and left the office in a stumbling run. And Kirkpatrick watched her go with haunted eyes. The Great Dane turned its head and looked back at him and its lips lifted in a soundless snarl that showed gleaming white fangs.

NITA FLED to Wentworth's home, hoping against hope that she might find reassurance there. But Jenkyns' old eyes were swollen with weeping, and Ram Singh had already left for Dick's Long Island estate, there to gather his belongings and leave for India.

Nita, still refusing to believe, went to her home, with Apollo pressing ever close to her side. In her apartment, the girl threw herself down on her knees, caught the dog's great head between her hands and looked with brimming eyes into his face.

"But we don't believe it, do we, Apollo? Do we, boy?"

The dog whined low in its throat, licked out its pink tongue. Nita got slowly to her feet. She would not believe. She began feverishly to pack a small overnight bag, stopped a moment to repair the damage emotion had wrought on her face, and hurried out. She took a taxi to a garage and wheeled out the compact but powerful Renault that Dick had helped her select.

She sent it skimming over the roads, Apollo on the seat beside her, thrusting his head out from behind the windshield into the push of the wind. The swift drive over Queensborough bridge and out onto Long Island roads cleared her head.

Wasn't it possible that Wentworth had escaped? He was a superb swimmer and, unless he had been stunned in the plunge, unless he had wanted to die—Dick want to die? She laughed, and actual gaiety crept into her voice. He would risk his life gladly in any just cause, but it was because he loved so to live that he got pleasure in thus defying death.

It was an hour and a half later that she swung into the drive that twined, through trees, up to the home Dick had built on the hill, for the day, he had explained to Nita with a twisted smile, when some other man, stronger than himself and with an equal oneness of purpose, could take up his battle against the forces of evil. The day when Dick and Nita....

She choked on the thought, saw the old caretaker running

toward her, a man with a face the weather and sun had thickened like leather and seamed with good nature.

"Is Dick here?" she called gaily.

The man came smiling up to her, a battered straw hat in his hands, his overall knees smudged with dirt from his labors among the flowers.

"Ain't seen him this month, Miss Nita," he said. "And I've been wantin' to show him his peonies. They're gorgeous, ma'am. And that cross he worked out that I says wouldn't do a thing—Miss Nita, it's the loveliest flower you ever saw."

Nita's hope died. She had hoped that Ram Singh's coming here meant Dick had set up a secret domicile in this place.

"Then Ram Singh isn't here either?"

The man frowned a little in bewilderment.

"If the master ain't here, ma'am, why would—"

Nita nodded jerkily, her throat too choked for words. She moved a hand in farewell, spun the wheel and shot the Renault down the drive again with gravel-spurting tires. This place was too full of memories.

SHE TURNED back toward town. Perhaps she might run into Ram Singh on the road. Evidently, he had not yet had time to reach the estate. She forced herself to drive slowly and, passing brick columns beside the road, saw the name of MacDonald Pugh on a mail box. On an impulse, she spun the wheel and drove in. This was where Dick had mentioned coming for the week-end. Perhaps in this part of the country he expected to find some clue to the Black Death. Perhaps she—

Grimly Nita van Sloan decided that if Dick had died, then

she would devote the rest of her life, if necessary, to clearing his name of the smirching charge that he was the Master of the Black Death. For his identification as the Spider she had no apologies.

Nita had been nearer collapse than she had realized. But the determination strengthened her. She drew up before the house, and MacDonald Pugh, seeing her from the porch, hurried out to greet her. He was dressed in tennis flannels. His face and great bald head were redly sunburned. Even his big hands, clasping hers, were red.

"I'm damned glad you came, Nita. Of course this whole business about Dick is preposterous."

The girl smiled bravely with lips that quivered a little in spite of her. It was good to find someone who believed.

"Dick told me the other day you had asked us out for the week-end," she said. "I know he'd want me to carry on."

"Exactly," Pugh agreed. He caught up her grip himself and carried it into the house, walking beside her with his heavy, forward-thrust head bent attentively. "If you give way to grief, people might think you gave some credence to those ridiculous charges. The late papers practically refute them anyway. Have you seen them?"

Nita stopped, whirled toward him. Her lips dared not frame the question. Pugh's wide mouth turned down wryly.

"The newspapers got another letter signed the Black Death. Even if the Spider is dead, the letter said, the plague will go on unless the money is delivered. Good Lord," Pugh growled, striding on into the house. "As if the banks could shell out a billion dollars like so many rolls of pennies and not feel it. But they'll do it." His face went grim. "They'll have to, or else...."

Nita's shoulders sagged slightly. She had been hoping against hope that there might be some new information about Dick.

"But they haven't—" she hesitated, walking into the cool dimness of the hall, "they haven't—"

"They've found no trace of Dick's body, no," Pugh said kindly.

A maid came then and took over Nita's case and showed her up winding stairs to a coolly bright room. She dismissed the servant instantly and stood in the middle of the floor staring about her while the Great Dane prowled around, sniffing at everything and finally standing before Nita, peering up with lolling tongue.

Nita forced herself from the lethargy that kept dropping back upon her, opened her case and swiftly dressed in riding clothes. The clue she believed Dick sought might lie in the country about here, or it might lie among the weekend guests. But the guests could wait until night. She would have to do any exploring she was to accomplish at once.

A SHORT while later, she went alertly down the stairs, wearing khaki jodhpurs, a silk blouse that, open at the neck, showed the sweet curve of her throat and, drawn down over her rebellious curls, a soft brown felt. Pugh sprang to his feet as she came to the porch. He was alone there.

"The others took a spin down to the town for drinks," he said. "Katherine said she was damned sick of rye all the time and longed to taste some real bathtub gin again." He made a face, and Nita saw gratefully that he was religiously avoiding the subject of Dick, deliberately treating her as though tragedy had not a few hours before sought to tear her heart in two.

"Your wife has small cause to complain of your rye, Mac." She smiled up at him, then glanced down at her riding clothes. "I know it's the wrong time of day, but I wanted to take a ramble through the woods on one of those excellent riding horses of yours."

Pugh nodded instantly.

"I'm only sorry I can't accompany you," he said, "but I'm expecting someone from town. Business," he wrinkled his reddened face wryly. "Otherwise Dick and I would be trolling for tuna off Montauk.

"I'll go have a horse saddled for you," he broke off, turned and strode long-legged off toward the stable.

He was gone a considerable while, and Nita began to stroll down toward the red-painted barn herself before he came out of its dimness frowning.

"Something seems to have happened to all my good horses," he said angrily. "It looks as if that new groom has gotten poisoned weeds in with their hay. I've only got one to offer you, Nita, and he won't be very spirited. It's an old one I got for Katherine. She doesn't like them lively."

Nita nodded carelessly. "I'm sorry about your horses," she said. "If it wasn't that I'd set my heart on a ride—"

"Quite all right," said Pugh, and the stable boy led out a dappled gray horse to whose back he assisted Nita. Apollo threw up his head and frisked about like a puppy.

Suddenly the horse reared on its hind legs, pawing the air,

whinnied shrilly and flopped flat on its back. Only Nita's long experience and her swift leap saved her. She sprawled as her feet hit the ground, but she was up instantly.

The horse jerked up its head from the ground, tried to maneuver its legs, flopped back and, breathing hoarsely a few times, died. Nita stared at it with startled eyes, then walked about its head, cried out and pointed at the gray forehead.

"A bullet hole!" she gasped. "Someone shot the horse!"

CHAPTER 17
THE CAVE OF THE PIGEONS

MACDONALD PUGH was stunned for a moment. Then he crossed to Nita's side and stared down at the horse's head. Fury seized him, and his clenched teeth showed between his lips. But mingled with his anger was bewilderment.

"But why in the devil—"

Nita knew the answer, but could not tell him. She knew now that the clue she sought was in the country about Pugh's place. She did not know by what devious means Wentworth had fathomed the secret, but following in his intended footsteps, she had found danger. And that explained anew why he had asked her to feign a quarrel. It had been, too, at the same time he had announced his intention of coming to this place. And now, coming here, she found the horses poisoned. When she tried to ride the one that remained, it was shot! Could anything be clearer than that?

"I'll get the police on the trail of whoever dared to do that!"

Pugh swore. "It's damnable, shooting down a dumb beast like that. And he might very well have killed you, too!"

Nita laughed a little shakily.

"That thought has just this minute occurred to me," she said.

She walked slowly away toward the house, frowning thoughtfully down at the grass. Death had brushed her, but she was the more determined to investigate. She knew a thrill of excitement. This was how Dick had dared!

While Pugh stormed into the house, she had her Renault wheeled out and, climbing in, summoned Apollo to join her. It was only a few miles to Dick's estate, and he kept a stable there.

A half hour later, mounted on a thoroughbred that paced exuberantly across the fields, Nita loped off into the woods toward Pugh's place. Evidently his house was watched and near there she might pick up the trail of the man who had shot the horse. She wondered if it was because she, revealed now as the sweetheart of the Spider, was at the house that it was watched. She hoped fiercely that it was so. In the pocket of her jodhpurs rested the weight of an automatic. In the woods somewhere lay danger. But there also lay the trail to the man who had placed the onus of the Black Death upon the Spider.

Her excitement communicated itself to her horse. Its stride lengthened with the shaken reins and she whisked through the woods. Then abruptly she hauled back on the bit, brought the animal curveting to a halt.

On the opposite hill, perhaps a mile away, she had seen the brown flanks of another horse. She urged her own mount into the shrubbery and, rising in the stirrups, peered beneath a shading palm at that distant hill. The late afternoon sun probed its rays into the foliage of the hill opposite, and once more she saw movement there, saw a horse with a man upon its back move across a small clearing.

Excitement raced through her veins and she felt her breath quicken. As she had told Pugh, this was no time for riding. It was late. Besides the land ahead was on Wentworth's own estate and beyond was Pugh's. There was no stable nearby from which the horse might come. The man must be a trespasser, and that meant—

Softly Nita called Apollo to her side and, keeping him close, pushed down the shadowed hillside toward the trail the mounted man followed.

ALL ABOUT her was the sunset beauty of summer woods. An oriole's evening warble was soft in the hollow. A faint breeze fanned her nostrils with the damp sweet odor of the rich earth. Somewhere near at hand a red squirrel chattered. But Nita noticed none of these things. Low upon her horse's neck, ready to clamp a hand upon its nose if, approaching the other animal, it sought to whinny, she urged forward upon the trail she hoped would lead her to the lair of the Black Death.

When she reached the spot where she had seen the mounted man, there was no trace of him except the hoof-prints of his mount in the soft mold. Calling Apollo softly, she dismounted and indicated the trail. Then she stripped a silk neckerchief, tied it to make a long leash and, fastening it to the dog's collar, remounted and urged him on the hunt.

Apollo tugged at the restraining silk, snuffed the ground and loped off through the woods. Nita was hard put to follow, but the hoofs of the thoroughbred were nearly soundless on the damp earth. She laid low upon its neck, and branches whipped past with the speed of her passage.

Small, bending trees switched her arms and brambles scratched her. She scarcely felt them, for Apollo strained steadily on the leash, dragging forward upon the hunt, his tawny body a perfect, powerful machine, running silently as he had been trained. Not until he sighted his quarry would he give tongue.

Many times Nita had ridden to the hounds, raced beside Dick for the honor of the brush. She had taken the hurdles with courage, but never had the chase been over such terrain as this. Uphill and down, a striding leap across a ravine, a choppy jump over a log, a poise and a twist sideways about a tree. Finally the frail leash parted in her hand and Apollo was off, a tawny flash.

Then, indeed, the race became furious. She shook out the reins, and the gallant hunter beneath her responded. She could feel the marvelous power of his stretch and recover. Wind sang in her ears. The branches became whips now. They stung her shoulders, ripped at the silk of her blouse. She jammed her hat tighter about her ears, crouched lower and let the horse run.

She spotted Apollo only occasionally now, but dared not call him back. At this furious pace, they must be rapidly overtaking the man ahead. Then suddenly she pulled strongly on the reins, brought her horse to a sliding halt. There it was, the deep rich bay of Apollo giving tongue. He had sighted the quarry!

Nita's breath was quick, her face intent, the lovely blue eyes narrowed with an expression of hate that would have shocked many of the friends who knew her in their conventional drawing rooms. Here was no society girl out for a canter. Here was a woman whose lover had been torn from her in disgrace, a woman upon the trail of her lover's foes!

Nita swung to the ground and led the horse into a dense clump of birches where the shadows were gathering swiftly. She loosened its cinches and, touching the gun in her pocket, moved swiftly off through the dusk of the woods.

Above, red sunset still tinged the treetops. But here below the dying light filtered through but dimly. Nita's blouse was torn. The right sleeve had been ripped loose at the shoulder and slit half its length. There was a scratch across the smooth white flesh, and the stinging red slash of a branch had marred her cheek. But there was a smile on her twisted lips and her eyes were bright and keen.

Ahead of her Apollo still gave tongue. Suddenly his deep bay broke off in snarling anger, then all was silent. The Great Dane was never noisy when he fought.

NITA BROKE into a run. The gun was in her hand now, clenched ready in a white fist. She sprang across a narrow stream, stumbled, recovered and raced on. The grade ahead was steep. Her run slowed to a rapid walk, and even that became difficult to maintain.

Footing was uncertain now, and the light was almost gone. Nita tripped over a vine, sprang up silently and hurried on. Her lips were open and her lungs panted for air. Ahead, through the trunks of the trees, she could see the crest of the hill against the sky, and it was empty of life. A great rocky eminence thrust upward just below its top and its jagged peak was like the masked face of a man.

Nita halted, tried to still her laboring breath, to listen. The evening hush had fallen upon the woods. The birds were silent. The insects had not yet taken up the orchestration of the night. Faint wind rustled through the leaves with a sound like men whispering. That was all. Yet somewhere near here, Apollo had bayed, had snarled in anger and charged.

More cautiously now, her eyes questing through the blackening night, Nita advanced. Had the great dog triumphed, bowled over the man she trailed! Or had her faithful Apollo been killed? Was that man even now lying in ambush for her among the shrubs and great fragments of rocks, that tumbled from that peak which was near at hand now, were strewn across her path?

The pulsing of her blood was a throbbing excitement in Nita's ears. She thrust the gun ahead of her and pushed on, jerked to a sudden halt. *What was that sound?*

It was soft and gentle, yet seemed to have strong volume. Hearing it, Nita wondered why she had not detected it before. It was such a sound as a church full of people might make whispering a prayer together. Each one made little sound, but together, the volume filled the vast vault of the building. But this was without sibilance. It was all round vowels in two tones, a—*a cooing!*

And in a flash, Nita knew. Somewhere near her, together in

the blackness, were vast numbers of pigeons! Kirkpatrick had spoken of pigeons in connection with the Black Death. Wentworth had sought a clue here, and she had followed a suspicious man to a hiding place that was filled with pigeons!

There could be one answer only to this. She had stumbled on the secret spot from which the Plague Master loosed the dread Black Death upon the city, sending the doom of thousands on the homing wings of flocks of pigeons.

A strong shudder shook Nita. Here all about her was probably the contagion of this terrible new form of the Bubonic Plague which killed so horribly. But Nita did not turn and flee from the terror of that discovery as another woman might have done, as indeed many men would. Instead, her face became drawn with the intensity of her determination. Holding the gun ready, she moved forward again—toward the cooing of the pigeons, toward the lair of the Black Death!

As she advanced, the soft, gentle sound grew louder. It was fantastic that their muted voices meant a horrible death. Yet she realized how efficient was the plan this monster had devised. For who would suspect that death hovered on their wings? Who but the Spider!

And who, discovering how the Master of the Plague operated, could turn aside the swift, homing flight of a flock. As well try to shut the air from the city!

A few might be killed; a flock might be turned aside for a while. But ultimately even their dying wings would speed them to their habitation in the city, and the Black Plague would stride grimly through the streets, touching this man and that, clutching its strangling fingers about a baby's throat.

GRIMLY NITA resolved that if she died in doing it, she would destroy these messengers of death, checkmate the Black Death. It was for the Spider.

"Dick," the girl murmured. "Dick."

And as if that word had been a magic talisman, it gave her strength. She moved on.

Then the shadow of a rock seemed to come to life! Nita fired as quick as thought, and a man cursed. Footsteps sounded behind her. She whirled, gun ready, too late!

Steel bands seemed to clamp about her arms from behind. Her wrists were pinioned at her sides. The automatic was wrenched from her hand. On the back of her neck was the panting of a man's hot breath.

"I've got the little hell-cat!" a hoarse voice grated in her ear.

"The she-devil!" cursed another voice. "She got me in the arm."

Footsteps approached, and a shadow loomed before her. A hand slapped her face violently, and she gasped at the pain.

"Lay off that!" the man behind her rasped.

Another blow. Nita kicked out with her riding boot, and a man howled in agony. The shadow danced before her.

"Good for you, baby," said the man who gripped her.

She struck backward at him with her boot. But her heel thumped against a rock and the man laughed—then snarled.

"Cut it out, Bill," he ordered. "Served you right. Now lay off that and help me tie her up."

Ropes bit into her wrists then. The man she had kicked yanked them savagely tight, cursing at the pain his arm caused him.

"Hurt you bad, Bill?" asked the man who still held her from behind.

"Not as bad as I thought," the man grumbled, trapping her kicking feet and tying those, too. "Bullet just burned my arm."

He finished binding her and the two men, one at her feet, one with his hands beneath her arms, carried her through the darkness toward the sound of the pigeons, until the cooing became like the washing of soft waves that blurred all other sound.

Echoes clapped back the footsteps of the men then. They rang hollowly, and she realized that she had been carried into a cave. Her feet were dropped, she heard a match scratch, and an end of candle flickered into yellow light.

She stared about her. The walls were lined with coops of pigeons. The stench was sickening. The men who had captured her were roughly dressed, and handkerchiefs hid their faces. One had blood on his left sleeve, and he glared at her hatefully.

Nita was suddenly aware of her torn blouse, of the low V of the collar which had been ripped. Suddenly the other man strode across to the one he called Bill.

"None of that," he snapped. "We gotta wait and see what the boss says do. You get out and make sure that dog is dead. You hit him an awful wallop, but them things are tough to kill."

Bill glared at him. "And leave you in here with her, huh? I ain't quite that big a fool!"

The two men glowered at each other. Then the larger man, the one who had captured Nita, shrugged his shoulders.

"Okay," he said, "We'll both go."

They clumped off together, first blowing out the candle, and the echoing cave brought back their voices to her.

"Damn!" said one, "I'll be glad when we don't have to hear these damned pigeons all the time."

"It won't be long," the other muttered. "We'll turn them loose before long. Then we'll see about the girl."

"How long?"

"The plane with the money takes off at dawn. And about three hours after that—"

The man's voice trailed off into the distance, but there floated back to Nita's ears, as she lay helplessly straining at her bonds, the coarse laughter of the two men. It was lewd, suggestive.

Nita's eyes were wide with fear, and her face burned.

CHAPTER 18
DOOM OF THE PLAGUE

RANSOM PLANE TO FLY AT DAWN

IN NEW YORK CITY, miles from where Nita van Sloan struggled in terror against her bonds, thousands read the headlines and sighed with relief. It meant that the city had been forced by the threat of the Black Death to borrow a billion dollars from the banks, to place that money in a plane and start it off along the line the Black Death had charted.

If any other plane took the air, the Plague Master proclaimed, he would loose death upon the city.

So at Floyd Bennett field, out on what had been barren filled land beyond Brooklyn, men who moved like stooped gnomes in the weird, searchlight-cast shadows, fueled a black plane with silver wings. Suddenly the men whirled, staring off toward the long straight road that stretched to the city.

Sirens were purring there. One-eyed motorcycles droned, and behind them came swiftly a long line of armored cars. Troops patrolled the field, bayonets gleaming on rifles aslant their shoulders. One by one the armored cars rolled up to the black plane with its silver wings. The doors clanged open, and while men stood with drawn pistols, bundles of currency were transferred to the plane.

A billion dollars that would fly into the dawn sky to ransom a city from man-inflicted plague! The false dawn already showed in the east. In an hour would come the take-off.

And back in the cavern where the plague pigeons kept up their everlasting murmur, Nita van Sloan, who alone knew the secret of the cave, struggled futilely with her bonds.

Masked in shrubbery, on a field not far from the entrance to that dread cavern, waited another plane, a ship that, mockingly, was painted all black, the plane the Black Death would fly. It was fueled and ready, a few moments of warming up, and it would bear the monster into the sky.

A billion dollars ransom….

In the close, murmurous darkness, Nita was suddenly still, straining listening ears. Was she overwrought from long waiting in the blackness, or was that a furtive footfall in the shadows? She scarcely dared to breathe. It would not be death that crept upon her. Death she could face, but those men....

More frantically than ever she sawed upon her bonds, tugging and straining. On came the footsteps. They had entered the main chamber of the cavern where she lay now and still they came on, softly and steadily. If the walls had not caught up and magnified the sound, if her ears had not become accustomed to the pigeons, learned to hear through their cooing, she would not have detected.

But, hearing it, there was nothing she could do but lie helplessly and wait. The footsteps were quite near now, almost beside her. In a few moments she would know. A scream rose in her throat, but she choked it down. A foot struck her leg.

Abruptly white light slapped her in the face. Her eyes flinched shut from the glare. From above came a gasp, and—

"Nita, Nita darling!"

THE GIRL caught her breath. That voice. It couldn't be! It was!

"Dick! Oh, Dick!" she sobbed.

Strong arms caught her up in the dark, a kiss brushed her lips, competent, swift fingers worked on the ropes that bound her. Loosed were her wrists, her feet.

"Dick," babbled the girl. "A light, I must have a light. Let me see you."

In the darkness Richard Wentworth laughed softly, and a

The two ruffians who had overpowered Nita came in now and rapidly bound Nita and Wentworth to a huge rock.

match flared. A candle took slow flame and he crossed back to where she still huddled on the floor.

"I'm sorry, darling," he murmured into her hair, holding her close against him. "I'm sorry, but there was no other way. I was afraid, was sure the police would be watching you in case they were not convinced of my death. Even the newspapers did not prove anything. Kirkpatrick might have told the reporters he knew I was dead so that he could capture me again."

Nita was sobbing unrestrainedly now. She had no words but his name.

"Shh! Stop now, dear," he soothed her. "You must get out of here at once."

Slowly she stifled her tears of happiness, smiled at him tremulously with wet eyes. She got up on numb feet, rubbing her rope-chafed wrists.

"I'm ready," she said. "Come on."

The Spider's smile was still on his face, but it fled from his eyes. "I can't go, dearest. There's work to do." He touched a black valise that stood beside his feet, which she had not noticed before. "But you must. Hurry, now. The Black Death and his men will be here any minute."

Slowly the girl crossed to him. She put a hand upon each of his shoulders.

"Dick," she said, "I'll never leave your side again until this Black Death is beaten, or until—until we die together."

Wentworth peered deeply into her blue eyes. There was no fear there, only a great love and a vast determination. He did not argue with her longer for he knew it would be useless.

"Very well then," he said. "Help me turn loose these pigeons."

He strode toward the nearest coop. Nita hung onto his arm.

"But the Black Death!" she gasped.

Wentworth turned and stared at her, then laughed softly.

"They haven't been given the germs yet," he told her swiftly. "The plague acts on them much more quickly than on humans. They will be infected only just before they are freed."

The pigeons were stirring restively in the light of the candle. Outside, the night was still pitch black. But already, distantly, a rooster was crowing, and there was a sleepy first twittering of birds. Wentworth picked up a coop, shouldered it and carried it out of the circle of light to the open, tore off the door and hurried back. Nita, at his side, told him how she had happened to be captured.

Wentworth nodded. "That explains the rifle shot I heard in the woods this afternoon," he said. "I couldn't figure what the man was firing at. But I followed him and found this place. I went back home to get this valise...."

"We must have passed in the woods!" Nita cried.

Wentworth stopped on his way back for the third coop of pigeons, placed his hands on her shoulders.

"Darling, won't you go?" he pleaded. "Believe me there is more danger here than there was when I sent the car diving off Brooklyn Bridge, hung on to the wheel and let it drag me down."

Nita smiled at him, made a little moue. "You know damned well I won't," she said quietly.

WENTWORTH SHOOK his head, still smiling, but there was grave fear in his eyes. He knew that at any moment the super-criminal would come, and he must remain. He turned and strode into the cave again, Nita beside him.

"How far did you swim under water?" she demanded. "That was terribly dangerous, Dick."

"Dangerous?" A thin smile twisted his lips. "Yes, of course. Well, the current helped, dear. But if Kirkpatrick or his men had thought to investigate a crate that was floating down stream about fifty yards from them, they'd have found the Spider's head on the other side. I was lucky, Nita."

As he lifted another coop of pigeons, a grating laugh broke out behind them. It echoed horribly in the cave, and Wentworth, dropping the coop before him as a guard, whirled, but he saw at once that the shield was useless, for the masked man held a high-powered rifle that would drill through that frail covering like a sword through cheesecloth.

The man was high-shouldered, and a black hat drooped over his forehead. When he spoke it was with the evil, taunting politeness of the Black Death.

"You used the right tense, Wentworth—or do you prefer to be called the Spider?—I refer to your last sentence. You *were* lucky, but that—" he laughed horribly—"that is all over now."

Wentworth let the coop slide to the floor. He straightened, with his arms hanging at his side and his right foot pressed against the side of the valise that lay on the floor. Nita saw and hoped there was a weapon there—some new device of Dick's clever friend, Professor Brownlee.

But nothing happened, nothing except that Dick, speaking

sharply, in a voice Nita hardly recognized because of its harsh vehemence, snapped out:

"Why do you continue to hide behind that mask? Do you think I am a complete fool? Can you imagine that the Spider doesn't know that the name of his enemy is—" Wentworth paused, laughed shortly,—"is MacDonald Pugh?"

The man snarled behind his mask.

"That knowledge will do you no good, Mr. Spider. I do not intend to leave any witnesses to accuse me of the Black Death."

Slowly he raised his left hand and took off his black hat, ripped off the mask. Nita expected Dick to fling himself forward then, during the instant the man's eyes were covered. But Wentworth made no move, only stood with his gleaming eyes fixed on the face of his erstwhile friend.

Wentworth smiled calmly.

"I know all about you, Pugh," he said in his harsh, accusing voice. "Know how you framed that girl, Virginia Doeg. Know how you involved young Jim Handley. Know why you—"

"Brilliant, positively," sneered the man behind his rifle, and his usually pleasant face was twisted into a mask of hate. "You astound me, Spider. You've learned much since we met in Harper's office."

Wentworth laughed tauntingly. "And I fooled you there. Have you figured yet how I called the police and escaped?"

Pugh flung back his laughter at him. The sound was abnormally loud in the enclosed space. "Have you figured yet, how I managed to get away after putting your ridiculous Spider seal on the foreheads of those police?"

Nita stared from one of the men to the other. Why in heaven's name was Dick standing here bandying words with this criminal? Was he playing for time? Was help on the way? She felt a small thrill of hope.

WENTWORTH'S REVELATION that Pugh was the Black Death had startled her, but now she saw the entire trail plainly. The forgery had been committed in Pugh's office. The earlier conflicts had centered about the girl, Virginia Doeg. And when the Spider finally had wrested her from the super criminal, there had been another trail from the same spot, the trail of Jimmy Handley....

"...Jimmy Handley," Wentworth was saying. "I know that you framed him lest I should suspect you when I traced Virginia Doeg. But what I don't see is how you managed to kidnap that girl from the Marlborough, killing those three policemen...."

"It is enough that I did it," MacDonald Pugh snapped. "Enough of this talking! I have work to do." He raised his voice. "Bill! Dan!"

The two ruffians who had overpowered Nita came in now and at Pugh's orders rapidly bound Nita and Wentworth to a huge rock. Pugh placed an empty coop in the middle of the cave, and from each of the other crates against the wall extracted two birds which he placed inside this one wired cage.

He was in high glee, chuckling as he went about his work. As soon as he had taken two birds from a coop, the men dragged it outside. It was still dark there, and the pigeons moved restively but did not take wing.

"You get the idea, don't you, Spider?" he jeered. "Surely your brilliant mind can follow me. From each flock I take two pigeons, the others I turn free. But when these two fly to join them—" he stroked the head of one of the pigeons in his hand, "they will carry with them the virus of the Black Death. What a welcome they will get!"

Finally the work was completed, and Pugh came to gloat over his two helpless captives. He smiled at them gently.

"Ah, love," he said, and laughed like a fiend. "I want to leave you with something to occupy your minds, lest you grow weary with waiting for death. When I fly to collect the ransom money, I shall carry with me the pigeons from each flock. And when I have the billion dollars, I shall release them!

"I am afraid the city will be too busy fighting the plague to give much thought to pursuing me." He snarled suddenly. "America, bah!" he spat out. "How I hate it. But this plague will help to humble it, and in the end, when my own land whistles, America will come to heel."

"Your country?" Wentworth asked slowly. "And what is that?"

The man threw back his head and laughed. "America will learn," he said.

Nita shuddered at the sound of his mirth. It was unholy.

"But surely," she said, "Surely, you would not doom an entire city...."

Her voice trailed off. She knew he would. Pugh turned his vulture-like head toward her.

"There is another pleasant thought for you to wait with," he snarled. "Your dog is not dead. He recovered consciousness last night, but rather than kill him I drugged him for a few hours. Any moment now, he will wake up. He will be very thirsty. But see what an humanitarian I am! I have left water for him, a full pan of it!"

Wentworth frowned up at the tall, shoulder-hunched figure. What was the madman driving at?

"Ah, but I see I puzzle you, Spider," Pugh said, smiling terribly. "Very well, I will explain. Primer English for primer minds. When the dog wakes up the dog will be thirsty. The dog will drink the water which the man has left for him. And when he has drunk the water he will look for his master. And he will come to his master and lick the master's face. The dog will not know that the water he has drunk has in it—"

Pugh paused, gloating over the two. Wentworth's eyes widened slowly with horror. Words struggled to his throat.

"Not that," he pleaded. "Or kill me that way if you will, but not, not—"

"Not the lady?" Pugh supplied. "Ah, but you would deprive yourself of her company for many hours. Once more I must point out to you, Spider, that you are scarcely complimentary to the young lady. The Black Death, you know, takes about twenty-four hours to kill."

Nita cried out, "The Black Death!"

"Yes," smiled Pugh. "The dog will not know that the water has in it the germs of the Black Death."

He turned and strode from the cavern, laughing, and the walls echoed with the horrid sound. It rang in the ears of the two who lay waiting for the Black Death.

OUTSIDE THE paean of the birds increased. The mouth of the cavern faced the east; and Wentworth, raising his head, could see the first gray edge of the day thrusting palely above the horizon. He saw something else, too, saw the huge, hunched body of a great dog, of Apollo, reel up with drooping head.

Wentworth turned to Nita, looked at her with eyes that smiled tenderly.

"Darling," he said, "I begged you to go. You refused, even, you said, if it meant your death."

The girl met his gaze bravely.

"Yes, Dick."

Wentworth's smile grew twisted.

"The time has come," he said with slow words, "for the Spider to die. Out there Apollo has wakened. He must be drinking the germs now. You know that if I order Apollo to stay away, he will do it. And presently he will crawl off to die, and eventually you and I would go free."

"Yes, Dick, I know that." The girl's voice was grave. A courageous smile was on her lips.

"You know, too, dear, that if I call Apollo here, his sharp teeth will soon sever these ropes, that then you and I can get my plane, kill Pugh and save the city from the Black Plague."

"Yes, Dick, I know that." There was no break in Nita's words.

It was Wentworth's own voice that cracked, not for himself, but at the thought of this dear loved face dyed with the horrid blush of the Black Death.

"Darling," said the Spider, "shall I call Apollo—or order him away?"

The girl's smile never faltered. She puckered her lips and whistled.

"Here, Apollo!" she called. "To me, Apollo."

And even the Spider, who knew and loved her, who understood her as no one else in the world, marveled at the clear courage of her voice. Her voice was as soft, as gentle, as if she called a child to her lap, instead of summoning the dread specter of the Black Death.

Wentworth, raising his head again, saw the dog throw up its head, spin drunkenly and come at a stumbling run into the cavern. He plunged toward them with lolling tongue, the tongue that so recently had lapped up the germs of the Black Death!

"Down, Apollo!" Wentworth ordered sharply.

The dog stopped, stared at Dick and crouched slowly. Wentworth tugged as far away from Nita as their short bonds would permit, held out his bound hands behind him toward the dog.

"Apollo," he called sharply. He waved his bound hands the few inches the ropes permitted.

It was a game to the dog. They had played it before against some such emergency as this. But Wentworth had never thought that those sharp fangs, gnawing at the thongs, might mean death to him as well as freedom.

The instant his hands were free, he ordered the dog sharply away, bent and untied his ankles. Then, snatching up the valise, he turned and smiled at Nita, across the width of the cave.

"Good-bye, darling," he said.

"Dick!" the girl cried wildly.

Wentworth shook his head slowly.

"I have risked your dear life as much as I will," he said. "If I unbound you, I could not keep you from coming. I will send Ram Singh to free you."

HE TURNED and stumbled from the cave, tears blinding him. He could not even kiss Nita good-bye, lest already the loathsome contagion was at work within his blood, lest he pass on to her the Black Death.

And then, in the entrance of the cavern he paused, staring at an upset tin pan, at sand that had soaked up water, at Apollo far down the hill lapping eagerly from a creek. Carefully Wentworth examined the ground. The sand had almost dried again. There were no dog tracks beside it as there would have been if Apollo had stopped to drink water there. But there was the heavy print of a man's shoe and scuffed sand!

One of the men in leaving the night before, either deliberately to torture the animal, or blindly in the dark, had kicked over the carefully set pan of water, and Pugh had left without noticing! Probably he had given that spot of contagion a wide berth as he had gone toward his plane to fly for the ransom money.

Wentworth leaped to his feet and raced back into the cave. Nita, sobbing, cried out to him.

"I knew you couldn't leave me. I knew you couldn't!"

Rapidly untying her bonds, Wentworth explained what had happened, that they were saved from the danger of the Black Death. Together, then they raced from the cave, down the hill, hurrying toward Wentworth's place. In the hollow there was a crude cabin. As they crashed heedlessly through underbrush, they heard a man's voice cry out and, Wentworth, hurrying forward found a young man bound hand and foot beside a small coop of pigeons.

Wentworth knew what that portended. Another fiendish trap of MacDonald Pugh. He caught the man under the arms, dragged him to the open and freed him, asking meantime who he was.

"Handley," said the man, "James Handley."

Wentworth smiled grimly. That explained it. This was the fiancé of Virginia Doeg, the man who had been framed by Pugh to throw the trail away from himself.

As he worked on the ropes, he spoke swiftly.

"When I have freed you, I'm going to run like hell. I've got to overtake Pugh before he can release pigeons and turn loose the Black Death on the city. As soon as you can move about, kill those pigeons in there and burn the shack. My home is a little over a mile due east of here. Head for that, and I'll leave word for you to be taken care of."

As he finished speaking, he unfastened the last thong about the man's wrists, sprang up and ran off to where Nita was toiling up the hill. The man shouted thanks after him. Wentworth waved a hand and saw Nita plunge into a thicket of birches, heard the whinny of a horse and gave a great cry of hope. He had been afraid the mile of woods between the cave and his home would doom their chances of saving the city. But with the horse—

Nita already had tightened the cinches when he raced up to her. He sprang to the saddle, caught her up behind him and gave the thoroughbred his head. The animal had suffered no great discomfort except a lack of water, but there was no time to wait for that now.

Crashing through shrubbery, ducking under swooping tree branches, they raced back to Wentworth's home, the tawny form of Apollo a flash in the distance ahead of them, the black valise still clutched in Wentworth's hand.

STRAIGHT TO the hangar that housed his always ready plane, Wentworth galloped the horse. He sprang to the ground and with Nita close behind him, darted to the wide, sliding doors, threw his weight against them. While Nita completed their opening, he vaulted into the cockpit, touched the starter button.

Compression whined, the propeller moved slowly, and suddenly the motor caught with a coughing roar. The girl clambered up the wing, the slipstream whipping her hair about her face, completing the ruin of her blouse. Wentworth jerked the throttle, and the ship trundled out onto the field. He whirled it into the wind and, chancing the danger of a cold engine, sent the ship racing down the runway, took the air like a bird.

It was a speedy Northrup, a special plane with an adjustable pitch propeller, and it glittered, as scarlet as one of the Spider's own seals, as it swept in a steady climb upward, banked sharply and streaked off on the trail of the Black Death.

Wentworth knew the course that the money plane was scheduled to follow, guessed that Pugh planned to attack it. Pugh had ordered all planes from the sky on pain of releasing the Black Death. And Wentworth, turning the controls over to Nita—it was a dual control plane for long flights—swept the sky with glasses.

For long moments as they raced toward the city, he could see nothing. The haze of smoke above Manhattan's towers intervened. But once the scarlet streak had dipped through that and the course swung westward and north along the Hudson, he tried again with the binoculars.

The early sun was behind them, and suddenly Wentworth caught a flash of light. He focused the glasses more sharply and made out the silver wings of the ransom plane. Even as he watched, a small black plane swooped out of the clouds above it.

Wentworth's hands tensed upon his glasses. His eyes glinted. There before him was the plane of the Black Death!

Far up the river he saw the two planes slant downward together. They disappeared behind trees. The scarlet Northrup droned on. It was equipped with no machine gun, but in a compartment beside him Wentworth had a "Tommy," a Thompson sub-machine gun that would be wonderfully effective at relatively close range.

Grimly now, as the plane swept on, he unfastened the straps that held it and drew the gun up past his chest and above the cowling. He fastened it down with another strap, then wriggled into a parachute. After which he took the controls while Nita availed herself of similar protection.

Wentworth was ready for the battle. They were near at hand now, only a mile or two from the spot where the two planes had settled. And even as he watched, the black craft of Pugh shot above the tree tops and began to climb steeply. A moment later they flashed over the field and Wentworth, peering down, made out the inert bodies of three men stretched beside the silver-winged ransom plane.

Wentworth's mouth went grim. He unstrapped the machine gun and held it ready in his hands. Only a few hundred yards separated him now from the Black Death. Suddenly the plane ahead vaulted upward in an inhuman turn and shot back to meet him, with a flicker of flame behind its propeller that he recognized with mounting anger was a double machine gun. Where in heaven's name had Pugh got a military plane?

But there was no time to speculate on that. He must destroy the man. Wentworth had been watching keenly, and he had seen no pigeons winging back toward the city. He was positive the dread harbingers of the plague were still aboard.

He raised a hand to signal Nita to give him the controls, but the girl had already thrown the ship into a twisting spiral, dodging from the line of Pugh's fire. Pugh veered to meet them, and she whipped the nose back the other way. And now the black ship was within range of Wentworth's lighter gun.

PUGH WAS still struggling for altitude. Abruptly Nita let him have it. Instead of climbing, she put the Northrup into a steep dive, swishing down across the black ship's nose before Pugh could bring his guns to bear.

The killer flipped up the tail of his ship, but it was too late. The scarlet Northrup had darted under, and a stream of .45 caliber bullets ripped into the motor and underside of the black ship.

His fist struck the wrist of the other's gun hand.

Nita zoomed, Immelmanned and flashed back upon the tail of the black plane. But there was no need of further firing. Black smoke and a burst of flame ripped from the engine of Pugh's ship. Wentworth saw the Plague Master pumping frantically with a fire extinguisher.

The flames blossomed into full flower, flicked back at Pugh. He threw up his arms. The motors drowned the sound of his shriek. He reared for an instant in the cockpit, then leaped far out, clear of the flaming black plane. His parachute whipped open.

Without an instant's hesitation, Wentworth leaped, too, dropping the gun back into the cockpit, depending on the automatic in his pocket. But instead of jerking his rip-cord immediately, Wentworth let his body hurtle downward unchecked. He shot past Pugh like a bullet and fancied he heard a strangled cry of rage from the man.

A thousand feet from the rolling farm land beneath him, Wentworth yanked the rip cord. His parachute snapped open and he drifted downward, seeming scarcely to move. He could not see Pugh now. The man was hidden by the open bell of his own parachute. But the Black Death would not escape him.

Already the plague had perished in the flames of the ship, burning fiercely in a nearby field. And Wentworth would reach the ground first. He would be free of his parachute and ready, when Pugh landed, to exact vengeance for the hundreds who had died.

The ground sprang up beneath him and, flexing his knees, Wentworth spilled down on the soft earth, tugging at the windblown parachute. In a few moments, he was free of it and peering upward, spotted Pugh. He was sideslipping his parachute, putting as much distance as possible between himself and the vengeful Spider.

But Wentworth paced him easily. He saw Pugh's automatic

flame in his hand, but he still pursued, dodging the hail of bullets that spat viciously into the dust of the field. He put his hand into his pocket for his gun. It was gone!

SOMEWHERE IN that frantic tumble through the air, it had spilled from his pocket. For an instant Wentworth checked, then he ran on more swiftly than before. Counting shots on Pugh, he estimated that at the present rate the man would exhaust his bullets about fifty feet above the ground, would be unable to reload in time.

But Pugh was canny. He held one shot. His parachute was only forty feet from the ground, now thirty, now.... Pugh bent his knees and took the landing perfectly, whirled with raised gun as Wentworth raced at him.

But Pugh had figured without the wind in his parachute. Even as he leveled the gun, the collapsing sail was caught by a gust.

Wentworth had crowded him too closely. He had not had time to free himself from the harness, and the tugging parachute jerked him nearly off his feet. Before he could recover his balance and fire, the Spider was upon him

His fist struck the wrist of Pugh's gun hand, knocked the weapon fifteen feet away. And then began a grim battle for life, the Black Death and the Spider, grim-faced and bleak-eyed, in the warm bath of the morning sunshine.

"The end, Pugh! The end for you!" Wentworth cried. And there was laughter on his lips—fighting, angry laughter. "Remember the dog? Even if you overcome me, you—"

Pugh's face blanched. "Good God!" he cried in frantic terror. "You've got the Black Death!"

Wentworth laughed again tauntingly. And suddenly Pugh turned and ran.

The Spider let him run a little way, dragging the parachute, working with desperate hands on the harness. And just as Pugh was almost free, Wentworth jumped on the parachute with both feet. The man was yanked to the ground.

He scrambled up, tore off the last of the harness, and the Spider sprang upon him, seized him by the throat. Pugh struck in a frenzy of fear with his fists, but his blows were weak.

In the end, the Black Death was a coward and died a coward's death, with terror in his eyes, with the Spider's fingers crushing the life slowly out of him.

Wentworth rose from the body of the man with disgust mingling with the ferocity of his hate. He brushed his hands, reached into his trouser pocket and brought out the crude imitation of his own cigarette lighter with which Pugh had sought to incriminate him.

With it he printed upon the great bald head the vermilion death seal of the Spider.

Then abruptly he shot a glance upward, hearing the whistle of wind on a swooping plane. The scarlet Northrup glided in to a perfect landing, its wing slots cutting its terrific landing speed to a mere forty-five miles an hour. The slots were still in an experimental stage. But Wentworth had contrived to have them installed on his plane, and they worked perfectly.

Wentworth glanced once more at the man who had paid the

penalty at last for his crimes, then turned and loped toward the plane. But Nita did not wait for him. She whirled the ship and taxied swiftly in his direction, pointing toward the woods a few hundred yards distant with an outflung hand.

Then Wentworth saw that Nita had maneuvered the lever which hid the plane's license number on wing and tail with a thin layer of cloth on which a fictitious number had been painted, and he sprang to the wing.

Even as his feet touched, Nita jerked open the throttle, and the ship's wheels left the ground before Wentworth was settled into the cockpit. Then, peering over the side of the swiftly rising plane, he saw the need for haste. Bluecoated policemen were rushing onto the field from the woods, and guns glinted in their hands.

The seal of the Spider, they would find, but—Wentworth threw back his head and laughed, turned and blew a kiss to Nita—*the Spider was gone.*

CHAPTER 19
KIRKPATRICK IS GENEROUS

THE SPIDER was gone, yes. But that seal would tell the world that the Spider was not dead, that he had escaped the grave that had threatened in the river. And once more police, now that the Black Death was finished, would be able to turn their attentions to catching him.

Wentworth dared not go to his home, lest they be waiting for him there. Nevertheless when Nita and he drove back to the city in her speedy little Renault, the Spider, having sent Ram Singh on ahead with the small black valise and some private instructions in Hindustani, turned downtown and headed directly for police headquarters.

"Dick!" cried Nita, grabbing his arm, "Are you crazy? Have you forgotten…."

Wentworth smiled at her, stopped the car before police headquarters and kissed Nita for all the world to see.

"No, darling," he said, "It is you who have forgotten."

And he led the puzzled and still reluctant girl to the office of the police commissioner. An officer sprang up smartly and swung open the door, ushering into the presence of Stanley Kirkpatrick, the Spider and Nita van Sloan.

Nita stared in bewilderment at the three persons she saw there. Virginia Doeg, a young man she didn't know, but whom Wentworth bowed to and addressed as Handley, and Commissioner Kirkpatrick.

Kirkpatrick's face was grave, but years seemed to have dropped from him. His clothing was immaculate again, his black mustache was waxed to needle points, and he bowed with a gallant gesture to Nita.

"I have already communicated with the newspapermen," he said gravely. "They will be here in a few minutes."

"But I don't understand," Nita whispered to Wentworth. "What is this all about?"

Wentworth smiled down at her.

"Let Kirkpatrick have his fun," he said.

The door opened again and the newsmen filtered in, a keen-faced dilapidated lot.

Kirkpatrick greeted them somberly. One of the newspapermen nudged another.

"The Spider," he whispered, and all eyes riveted on Wentworth.

He pretended not to hear, but Nita's hands gripped his arm until her fingers ached.

"I called you gentlemen in," Kirkpatrick said, "to hear a dictograph record which was delivered to me today by the Spider—" Kirkpatrick looked up at the newsmen with a slight smile—"though not in person. But he called me up in advance and told me it was coming, and a taxi driver brought it."

He stooped and lifted to the table a rusty valise. He opened it, and gleaming metal showed inside.

"If you press the side of this bag," Kirkpatrick said, "it starts the machinery going, and a magnifying device which is the cleverest bit of work I've ever heard of, picks up any sound within a radius of ten or fifteen feet perfectly... I want you to hear the record."

HE PRESSED the side of the bag at the point he had indicated, and suddenly a harshly vehement voice spoke from the bag with a tone so life-like that Nita started:

"Why do you continue to hide behind that mask? Do you think I am a complete fool? Can you imagine that the Spider doesn't know that the name of his enemy is—" a short laugh barked from the instrument—"is MacDonald Pugh."

And another voice snarled out, the voice of a man they all knew to be dead, the voice of MacDonald Pugh.

"That knowledge will do you no good, Mr. Spider. I do not intend to leave any witness to accuse me of the Black Death."

And Nita, her heart singing, recalled that long talk she had not been able to understand in the cavern and remembered that it cleared her Dick in every particular, of every crime that the police laid at his door. She smiled gaily.

"Why didn't you tell me?" she whispered into Dick's ear.

"When?" He merely framed the word with his lips, and Nita, remembering, laughed. When would he have had a moment to tell her before they had landed again at his estate and started back over the road to town? And really this was much nicer than being told.

She heard, as in a dream, Wentworth's voice grating as it never naturally did and realized that he had been disguising his tones there in the cavern. Then Kirkpatrick stopped the machine and turned toward Wentworth.

"It's very obvious, Dick," he said, "that the Spider's voice is not yours. But that eccentric gentleman left nothing to chance. He told me over the phone—" He smiled and drew toward him a slip of paper. "I think I have the exact words. 'I do not appreciate your confusing me with that numbskull, Wentworth. He's all right, but he hasn't the brain for this type of work!'"

Wentworth was angry.

"That's all very well for the Spider to brag," he said vehemently. "I was on the right trail, though. He just beat me to it."

"That's right, Wentworth," jeered a reporter. "He just beat you to it."

And the newspaper men made a concerted dash for the door

to phone in the biggest story since five hours ago when the Master of the Plague had died.

Virginia Doeg and Jimmy Handley were the next to go. Handley stopping to shake Wentworth's hand, and say again the "Thank you," he had shouted when Wentworth had saved him. Then only Kirkpatrick and Nita and the Spider were left.

Wentworth crossed to the desk and held out his hand. Kirkpatrick gripped it fiercely, and the men's eyes locked affectionately. Nita, who could understand, slipped from the office, a soft smile on her lips. Finally the two men dropped their hands, a little embarrassed by their show of emotion.

The Spider cleared his throat. "That was generous of you, Stanley," he said, "making it as public as all that."

"Forget it," said Kirkpatrick shortly. "You have much more to forgive than I."

And he proffered his cigarette case. Wentworth accepted one, and with a quick gleam in his eyes, dug from his pocket the clumsy lighter that Pugh had made, the lighter which even now bore the seals of the Spider—seals that would not dissolve in an unknowing hand.

"I wonder," said Wentworth slowly, his tip-tilted brows mocking, "if you'd let me have that dictating machine as a souvenir of a case on which the Spider beat me to the kill?"

He flicked flame to the clumsy lighter with its Spider's seals and touched it to Kirkpatrick's cigarette.

POPULAR PUBLICATIONS

HERO PULPS

LOOK FOR MORE SOON!

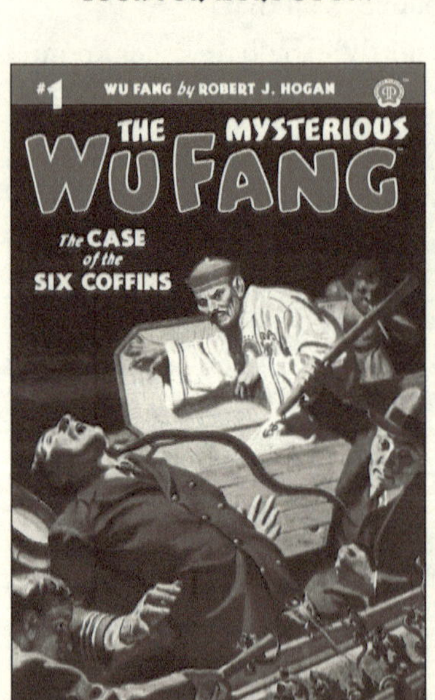

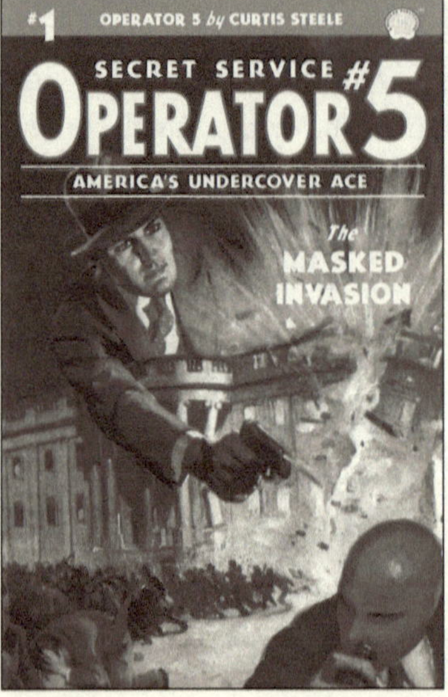

www.ingramcontent.com/pod-product-compliance
Lightning Source LLC
LaVergne TN
LVHW090944080826
845145LV00003B/882

* 9 7 8 1 6 1 8 2 7 3 7 9 6 *